Regby Dornik

The Chilling Warning

Garth Tuxford

Published by
Impressions Publishing
Tel: 01487 843311
www.printandpublish.co.uk

First Edition Published 2011

Printed and bound in Great Britain

A catalogue record for this book
is available from The British Library
ISBN 9781908374134

Acknowledgments

My sincere thanks to Bill Goss at IMPRESSIONS for his honesty and total commitment in helping a first time novelist achieve his goals. Sometimes my questions must have brought a smile to his face as I really had no clue where to start; he was patient and led me through each phase and I was humbled by his genuine desire to help.

I would also like to offer my sincere thanks to Ruth who proofreads for Impressions and corrected my grammar, punctuation and layout. At nearly 65, I suppose school was a long time ago. What touched me most was that she not only read and corrected where necessary but made the following remarks on returning the manuscript to Impressions:

Hi Bill,

I enjoyed reading the author's comments on my work, much as I enjoyed reading his work.

Thanks to my Daughter Heidi Tuxford for the illustration on the front cover.

Preface

December 2089

In what I imagined were my last moments I thought of Lisa and our baby and that I would never hold her in my arms again or ever see the child that we had made. Childhood memories flashed through my tormented mind: Mum and Dad; and my days at school - oh, why hadn't I worked harder at school; I was broken, screaming in terror and demented. Everything went black.

I vaguely recall being half lifted and dragged and more terrifying thoughts pierced my already addled brain. Where were they taking me, where were my friends, was I about to enter a hell where pain would rack my body for eternity?

It took several minutes for my eyes to focus and I was still shaking convulsively, almost resigned to whatever was going to happen to me.

"Who are you?" I gasped in awe and fright. "Who are you?"

Perhaps it is now time to go back to the beginning of this story and explain the full details of who I am and why I am here...............

Contents

Chapter 1	My Early Days	1
Chapter 2	University Success	3
Chapter 3	The North Atlantic	5
Chapter 4	James Durbin	9
Chapter 5	Strange Samples	17
Chapter 6	Meeting Thabo	19
Chapter 7	Into the Hills	27
Chapter 8	Finding the Mine	37
Chapter 9	The Warriors' Ceremony	39
Chapter 10	The Himba	49
Chapter 11	A Threat from Washington and a Plan	56
Chapter 12	New Challenges in India	65
Chapter 13	Planning for the Mine	87
Chapter 14	Return to the Mine	114
Chapter 15	The Terror Below	133
Chapter 16	Recovering from the Ordeal	161
Chapter 17	New Plans	176
Chapter 18	A Very Special Day	186
Chapter 19	Cap'n Joe and *Latis*	191
Chapter 20	Enlisting the Royal Navy	196
Chapter 21	The Final journey	212
Chapter 22	Meeting Regby	218
Chapter 23	The Finale	249

Chapter 1 My Early Days

I am Petrey Jonesy, a geologist from a Nordic background. I was born and grew up in Selsey and obtained my degree in Geology at Aberdeen University. Both my parents were geography teachers and I imagine this was the reason I grew up with a fascination in this field. However, they did not have my drive and ambition to travel and take my geology with me.

My Father's brother, Carl, had worked in Africa in the mines as an engineer and had been killed in a cave-in along with 3 of his colleagues whilst I was still at school. None of their bodies had ever been recovered. They had sealed the mine and placed a plaque at the entrance with the names of those who were lost. I always thought that one day I would go and pay my respects at the place.

As a boy I had a fascination with rocks and stones and by the time I was 10 had a collection of them in my bedroom that I had collected from beaches, rock quarries and anywhere I could find them. It was almost an obsession and I needed to know how they got there and where they had all come from. They were of all different sizes, shapes and colours and I was intrigued, even at that early age, by the way they were formed and how the sunlight glinted on some of the faceted stones. I wanted to know how they had been formed and how they had arrived at the places I had found them.

I learned from my parents that many of them were millions of years old, some were volcanic and many others had been torn out of the ground during the glacial period. I grew up with an almost fanatical fascination with their formation and construction and a thirst for learning about their origins.

As a schoolboy I went on every school trip that gave me the chance to learn more about my hobby. As I grew older my obsession led me to become an avid rock climber and mountaineer so that I could get closer to my beloved rocks.

I suppose it was inevitable that I would ultimately become a geologist. It was almost as if my future had been “carved in stone”, if you will excuse the obvious pun.

Chapter 2 University Success

At university, my obsession was fuelled by a desire to find out more and more about the whole spectrum of rocks, and I excelled in both history and geography and all things that would feed my thirst. Unfortunately, there was a downside and I had little interest in other subjects, which of course I needed to achieve my degree.

Had it not been for a new lecturer recently arrived at the university I would have certainly failed my degree. Professor Crickley had a profound effect on my life and certainly crafted me as a successful geologist.

Very early on, he recognised in me something that he later confided to me was a condition that he himself had gone through at a similar stage in life. I don't know why he singled me out for special attention but looking back I am most grateful that he did. He made me realise how important a good grounding in maths and physics would be to my chosen career in Geology and anyway it was a compulsory part of the course. From then on, I devoted as much of my time and effort in all subjects that would lead me ultimately to my degree in Geology.

Professor Crickley had a great sense of humour and he always made learning an enjoyable activity. As I came to know him more I found out that he had recently lost the love of his life, his beloved

Gina and his wife of twenty-eight years had died very suddenly of a rare blood condition. Although he was bereft at his great loss, he had a beautiful nine year old daughter, Grace born on 14th September 2069 which was also her Mother's 41st birthday. He doted on Grace who, he said, was the best thing that ever happened to him. He became a very close friend and acted from then on as my mentor and he always managed to get the very best from me.

On completion of my degree course, I acquitted myself well and achieved an honours degree in Geology. Professor Crickley seemed almost as pleased as I was and wrung my hand warmly in congratulations on my achievement.

I was sorry to leave collegiate life and Professor Crickley was sad at my leaving. However, we had formed a strong bond and remained friends for many years. Somewhere along the line, I had dropped the Professor title and he had become Brendan. Grace had never been christened and Brendan paid me the great honour of inviting me to become Godfather to his darling Grace.

I always had this dream that I would discover something ground breaking, even sensational, but it looked as if my destination was not as exciting as my dreams and aspirations. I secured a well-paid job with Caltex and I put my expertise in Geology to good use. I received a number of accolades from the company as I seemed to recognise many commercial opportunities during my research into oil exploration. But somehow none of it lived up to my expectations. Perhaps I was searching for that fifteen minutes of fame, which I believed everyone would ultimately get.

Chapter 3 The North Atlantic

By the time I was twenty-nine I had become one of the foremost Geologists within the oil industry. I was well known to most of the major oil companies and had worked on joint ventures with most of my competitor's team of geologists. Then one day my life changed, not just a little bit but instantly and very dramatically.

During a time of hectic drilling many, many samples were brought to the surface and we came across a great number of anomalies which usually turned out to be fairly normal. However, on this particular day I did some quite deep analysis on some of our latest samples that had been sent to me from a drilling rig situated just to the west of Surtsey.

(On November 8, 1963, about 130 meters below sea level, off the coast of Iceland (63.4N / 20.3W), a new island began to form due to a submarine volcano. There was little to no coverage of the event at the time. Scientists followed it because scientists do that.

The eruptions of the submarine volcano became visible above the Atlantic Ocean on November 15, 1963. While Surtsey was forming, volcanic ash and smoke shot up to 10 kilometres above the vent of the island.

Volcanic ash clouds separate electrical charges just like vapour clouds so there were many lightning storms during the creation of Surtsey.

During the first few days, eruptions were not explosive and consisted of gentle effusions of pillow lava. As the volcano grew towards sea level, the water pressure decreased and activity became explosive.

The early phases of the eruption were caused by the interaction of magma and water (phreatomagmatic). Explosions were closely spaced or steady jets, producing dark clouds of ash and steam shooting a hundred meters above the vent.

On January 31, 1964, activity shifted 400 meters to the northwest and eruptions continued at a new vent.

As the eruptions progressed, a new tuff ring developed that protected the vent from seawater. On April 4, 1964, this caused the activity to change from phreatomagmatic explosions to lava fountaining and lava flows.

Lava flows extended the island to the south and protected it from wave erosion. This phase of the eruption ended on May 17, 1965. Surtsey was quiet for more than a year.

On August 19, 1966, activity resumed at new vents on the east side of the island. More lava flows moved to the south partially overlapping the older flows. The eruption stopped on June 5, 1967).

It is now 2085 and 118 years since this historic event and the island has continued to grow ever since. There are also many naturally formed tunnels on the island, or are they natural?

It was the North Atlantic and a very miserable stormy and cold October morning in the North Atlantic. I was looking forward to a long weekend ashore in Londonderry, Northern Ireland. As part of a joint survey with the Royal Navy, I was on board HMS Extra, a hydrographic vessel. It had now become commercially viable for the Royal Navy to work closely with civilians as it helped to fund the much-depleted service.

I had been aboard the Extra for a couple of months and this time of the year, end of October, it was extremely dangerous and many times we had to tie ourselves into our bunks to avoid being pitched onto the lurching deck. The chef often found it difficult to prepare any food because his galley did not stand still long enough for him to get any cooking done. We ate a lot of bread and cheese at these precarious times.

We had been at sea for several weeks now and much of the research had been mundane, with no new findings We were due to anchor in Loch Foyle in a couple of days and I thought that a steady laboratory would make any work much more pleasant and the thought of terra firma for a few hours in the evening was a real joy. A stroll through Londonderry was always pleasant and the some of the boutique restaurants nearly made all that time at sea worthwhile.

For a few minutes I was lulled into thoughts of cold beer and warm food.

What the hell was that? I was brought suddenly and violently back to the present loud juddering crashing sound reverberated round the ship. My immediate thought was that we had been in a collision with another vessel. As we continued to lurch and surge in the stormy conditions, I clawed my way up the ladder to get to the upper deck and find out exactly what was happening.

The Captain and half of the ship's officers were on the Bridge and there was a lot of shouting and arguing going on. I managed to get a good look around but nowhere could I see any sign of the vessel I thought we must have hit. Soon it became clear amongst the chaos on the bridge that nobody appeared to know what we had been in collision with, there was much speculation and many of them thought that it was a submarine of some sort.

The hydrographer said he was sure that it wasn't a rock or a piece of land as the surveying equipment was still steadily churning out the lines of the bottom which was about 2000 feet deep.

It felt very strange that evening as the half-light rapidly descended into arctic darkness. So far, we still had no idea what had caused the collision. A hole of about 5 feet by 6 feet had been torn out of the ship's side just below the waterline and the shipwright and his assistant worked rapidly to place a large tingle over the damaged area. It was nearly midnight before a very wet and bedraggled shipwright completed the temporary repair to the damaged ship's side. He was in desperate need of a large tot of rum and the chef managed to cook up something warm for him to eat.

I was curious to chat to him about the damage as were several other officers, including the Captain, and so I had to wait until late the following afternoon before I managed to question him.

Chapter 4 James Durbin

James Durbin, Lieutenant Shipwright, was an intriguing man and had been in the Royal Navy for twenty-five years, starting as an Artificer and then being commissioned early at just twenty-six years of age. He was never married and always said that the sea was his Wife. He had been commended for his action during the Reykjavík incident back in 2072 when he single-handedly removed an unexploded missile from the cable locker of HMS Divine, the only remaining Destroyer on the North Atlantic Patrol.

It was rumoured that the missile had trapped five sailors in the cable locker and James Durbin had kept them entertained with his sharp wit and humour during their traumatic experience. He managed to keep them upbeat when under the most arduous of conditions, and whilst his own life was in jeopardy he cheerfully cut the still live missile out of the metal structure of the cable locker.

He joked that only the good die young and he was far too wicked to be taken in such an inglorious manner. He told the young frightened sailors that they would all live to be grand old men and would retell this story with many embellishments to their young grandchildren.

Those young sailors certainly did live to tell the tale and all were grateful to the young Lieutenant who had not only saved their lives but gave them hope that they would live.

It was this gregarious Lieutenant that I wanted to talk with, in detail, about his latest escapade aboard the Extra. I was way down the list of priorities when it came to talk with him; after all he was a serving Royal Navy officer and I was a civilian geologist whose company paid for the privilege of using their ships and facilities.

The Captain made the decision to head for Londonderry immediately where we could put into effect proper repairs to the damaged hull. After all, James Durbin's immediate first aid repair would not last long in the mountainous seas of the North Atlantic in autumn, and even he knew that. Also, the Captain did not want to hurry because that could also have a devastating effect on the temporary repair job. So there we were, with high winds on our stern, bobbing and weaving our slow way back to Londonderry.

Late the following afternoon I met up with James Durbin and, although until now we had only been on nodding terms, we hit it off very well. Both of us enjoyed a sense of humour that often annoyed the more serious.

We swapped small talk for half an hour or so before bringing up the subject that I was so desperate to talk about. As a geologist, I really wanted to know if the damage had been caused by some sort of natural phenomena or by something man-made.

James said that from experience he thought that the damage had been caused by a man- made object as there were no signs of the usual debris associated with hitting the bottom, which was impossible where we were situated, or a volcanic vent which would still have left a great deal of debris. He also said that if it had been volcanic then there would have been a strong smell of sulphur in the air around the crash area, both by the hole and in the atmosphere around the ship. Nothing of the like had been reported and he had certainly not smelt anything whilst repairing the damage.

He had discussed the likelihood of it being some sort of submarine with the Captain who agreed that this was most likely and had contacted all the agencies to enquire whether they had any submersibles in the area. However, there was something he had not discussed with the Captain. He said that he was concerned about losing his credibility and so kept his thoughts to himself. He did not want to talk about it immediately but needed to collect his thoughts and reflect on it before making any rash statements.

I tried to push him for more information but he was adamant and asked me to be patient. However, he did promise that he would talk to me later once we were ashore in Londonderry and that he would talk to me first about it. He said that he would feel more comfortable talking to me about it than to any of the other officers, partly because I was a geologist, also because I was a civilian and would not ridicule him for sounding so preposterous.

He was not going to tell me anymore and there was little else I could do apart from making a start on some of the samples that had been sent to me from the drilling rig.

I had intended to leave this work until we were anchored but, with my thoughts full of other things triggered by the accident and James's curious findings; I decided to make a start on the samples.

It takes some time to fumble through all the pieces and most of them are the usual findings but every now and again I find the all-important signs of oil or gas, which is just as well or I wouldn't have any employment. I was slowly bagging up each sample with various tags and my findings for each one when I noticed a rather curious sample that seemed to be a reddish brown around the edges. This usually meant that the sample contained metal substances that were oxidising. But somehow this one looked a little different from any I had worked on before.

I set about scrutinising it with greater interest and the events of the day just dissipated, this was more like it, something out of the ordinary to get my teeth into and, hopefully, justify my salary.

Over the past 200 years or more there have been a number of studies of the formations found on the seabed in the North Atlantic and as part of my degree preparation I have read several of them. They get more and more technical as history unwinds but one of the most interesting was a book entitled,

> ***"The North Atlantic Seabed comprising A Diary of the Voyage On Board HMS Bulldog in 1860 and observations on the presence of animal life, and the formation of organic deposits, at great depths in the ocean".***

The following is a short extract taken from the daily diary taken on board HMS Bulldog.

In parts, the diary is difficult to work out but it makes little difference to the statements made on or about 11th October 1860.

> ***At Goodhaab I repeatedly came across small bergs in the fiords, laden with mud and detritus and sometimes carrying imbedded stones of moderate size. One of these I was induced to study more closely than perhaps I should otherwise have done. One of the most compact stones was a completely different colour to all the rest, what I would expect to be a normal glistening black was an ochreous yellow, caused by its long immersion in water and beneath the surface was a metallic like substance for which I cannot explain. It was a source of great interest but was never resolved"***

My imagination started to run riot and I found I was imagining all sorts of answers to the information that lay before me. I needed to calm myself down and try to think carefully about the evidence that I had here. I racked my brain to think of logical answers but could find none. I used Crypto, the latest in computer search engines available using my special password to access the most sensitive of information. This was a privilege afforded me when I became affiliated to the Royal Navy, having been seconded to them from Caltex. I found a few references to strange and unusual findings over the last 15 years or so and like the Bulldog ships log way back in 1860 there seemed to be no logical conclusions.

There are many discoveries that have no common answers that are just left hanging in the air, with current authorities believing that at some stage these phenomena will be resolved.

However, I was impatient and didn't believe in unsolved anomalies. I was determined not to let it escape me.

The weather continued to deteriorate. I was unable to continue with my research and gave it up for the day. I went to bed that night with my brain in turmoil and slept fitfully. I awoke from my disturbed sleep very early the following day, looking forward to the ship mooring in Lock Foyle. It was a slow and tedious journey to reach the North East Coast of Ireland and back into the protection of the River Foyle. Even when we arrived, the wind remained strong and we had some difficulty in navigating the small ship into the protection of the Lough.

Everyone on board seemed quite upbeat at the prospect of having a few days on 'terra firma' and the opportunity to savour a good meal and a foaming glass of real Irish Guinness.

I found James Durbin in the bathroom taking a shower prior to setting off ashore and we agreed to meet up at the River Inn and Cellars at about 8.30pm, the oldest bar in Derry.

Only a few minutes' walk from Foyle Embankment, the River Inn has been located on the boundary of the historic city walls since before the Great Siege of the 17th century and open to the thirsty public since 1864. The atmosphere was very cosy and the traditional pub grub was a welcome sight after our much restricted menu aboard.

There is so much history in this ancient town and I took the opportunity to explore the Tower Museum and a number of the still cobbled ancient side streets before making my way down to the River Inn to meet James.

He was sitting on his own close to one of the small shuttered windows and beckoned me to his table as I entered the bar. We ordered the special seafood platter which included French fries and brown bread and butter. We spent about 10 minutes in idle chatter whilst we waited for our food to arrive. Both of us seemed a little nervous about broaching the subject that was foremost on our minds.

I broke the ice and asked him if he had thought any more about the events of a couple of days ago. He said that he had still not spoken to anyone else about something that he thought was a little strange. Once I got him talking there was no stopping him, and he no longer felt embarrassed about talking to me.

James was completely convinced that the underwater collision had been caused by some sort of submersible craft. Round the edges of the hole in the ship's side was a substance that he could not identify. It was metallic and there were signs of oxidisation and also a bluish gooey substance which he also could not identify. I asked him if it was possible for him to get me a small sample and he agreed that he could. Then I asked him if he had any theories as to what had happened and what the craft was, but he said that he really had no idea.

The Captain made an announcement the following day that we would remain here for 6 days before resuming our patrol in the

North Atlantic, ample time to study the samples that James would get for me. I was starting to think that once I received the samples it would only take me a short time to discover what they were and it would just be a routine finding and would lead us to whoever the submersible had belonged to.

It was seven years since I had left University, although sometimes it felt like it was only yesterday. Whenever I could I would call Brendan and bring him up to date on all of my activities and where I was and what I was doing. I always enquired about Grace and I was quite surprised to learn that she had just celebrated her 16th birthday. I hadn't seen either of them for nearly five years and she was growing up very quickly. Like her father she was studious and had made up her mind that she too wanted to be a geologist. Unlike her father she did not want to be a classroom geologist but out in the field getting her hands dirty. Well, time enough for that as she still had two years' schooling to complete before starting her four year degree course in Geology.

As soon as I got back to the ship I called Brendan on my satellite phone and explained where I was and the reason for our stop in Londonderry. He was still teaching at Aberdeen and had a very modern high tech laboratory at his disposal. I can do many things on board with the equipment available to me but nothing as sophisticated as a University Lab. He said that if the samples proved interesting then I should send them to him and he would like to study them and give me his expert advice.

Later the following afternoon James, as promised, gave me the samples that I was quite excited about studying. He is no geologist but he was quite right that these samples were indeed strange. I carried out a few obvious tests on the metal like substance and there were traces of iron but what it was combined with was a mystery. Also the rubbery content appeared to be an adhesive lining to the torn metal. However, once more this was beyond my knowledge and local equipment and I realised that my only option was to hand the samples over to Brendan. I packed them up and was very reluctant to despatch them; I only did so after making sure that Brendan would keep his findings confidential.

Chapter 5 Strange Samples

I knew I was going to need to be patient as we would be off to sea again very soon and it would be several weeks before I could get up to see Brendan and hopefully his results.

As it happened things took a rapid change and the oil exploration team at Caltex had an urgent mission for me and arranged for me to be relieved by another geologist. I was given four days leave between departing HMS Extra and reporting to Caltex near Aberdeen. That was good because it allowed me to spend some time with Brendan and Grace at their home close to Aberdeen University.

Grace took me by surprise as it had been a long time since I had seen her and she was no longer the gawky little girl that I remembered. She was tall and very slim and was the spitting image of her mother.

She had so many of her mother's traits and mannerisms which was at times quite disconcerting as she had been quite young when her mother had died. Even the quizzical way that she looked at me and the gentle smile, was so like her mum. She also had the patience to hear everything I had to say before adding her own rhetoric. She was a delight to be with and was very pleased to see me and was very curious about the secret that her Father and I shared.

Knowing that my time with them was short, Brendan wasted no time in getting to work with the samples. It took him no time at all to ascertain that the main shell of whatever it was contained metal but it was mixed with other substances that he did not recognise. He had a colleague who was a Metallurgical Engineer who worked with a Materials Consultancy and Testing Company, which tested Physical properties, Chemical analysis, Elemental analysis, Thermal analysis and Porosity.

The test on both the metallic substance and also the rubber type covering proved very difficult to analyse. The findings were that neither were anything easily identifiable and the only conclusion was that it may have been part of some space debris, satellite or sputnik that had jettisoned into the sea having fallen out of orbit. This would make sense as new materials were always being produced on one of the space stations encircling the earth. Brendan's colleague offered to send the sample to Washington for further analysis.

So there it all ended for the time being and the wait went on. It was many months before I would know exactly what the submersible was made of, although it made perfect sense that it would be something that had dropped from the sky. The earth was littered with debris from used up and burnt out fragments and much of it fell into the oceans.

Chapter 6 Meeting Thabo

I enjoyed too few days with Brendan and Grace and all too soon I was off to Caltex to find out what this new urgent project was all about.

I didn't have to wait long and in less than two days I was on a plane on my way to South Africa. I was given a brief to read about the history and geography of the area I was going to work in. It was the site of an old open cast mine, the Kaolin mine at Fish Hoek.

There was a great deal of ancient history attached to this area and there were early signs of humans in the area as long ago as 400,000 years and even more modern man living in caves 25,000 to 30,000 years ago. Most of the mining had ceased many years ago and the area was now rich in vineyards that supplied wonderful quality wines to most parts of the world.

Fish Hoek was just fifteen miles from the Cape Town. The old Kaolin mine is situated some miles inland and is easily accessed in a 4 wheel drive vehicle.

I was overawed by the beauty of South Africa and the city of Cape Town which boasts an absolutely stunning beach. It had always puzzled me why my parents had never had the inclination to travel.

Apparently there had been rumours and speculation about a huge oilfield directly beneath our feet that spread out not only north under the surrounding hills but also south and directly under Cape Bay. I had been briefed and instructed to study the area and confirm or deny the existence of such a huge oilfield. Of course with all the modern technology, ground scanners and laser equipment it was far simpler to ascertain what lay beneath the surface than the old fashioned way of just looking for oil soaked rocks.

It soon became very obvious that there was something quite substantial beneath the surface. To write a report on such a large project I wanted to visit the surrounding hills and beaches and take my own soundings and sonic readings. An oil well of this size would be simple to access from the seas but I wanted to spend some time in the hills and try to get a feel for the enormity of it all.

Apart from the commercial stand, I really wanted to get close to these ancient hills and see what other secrets they might hold; particularly knowing that history had provided many hints as to what life had been like many thousands of years previously. It was also less than a hundred miles from the mine which had taken my Uncle and his colleagues and I was even more curious to carry out my research as far north as was necessary.

I remained close to the old Kaolin Mine for about a week poring over charts and maps and overlaying them with the ground radar that provided me with the extent of the oilfield.

Most of the work that I do is done in isolation and sometimes it can be quite a lonely task. However, I was fortunate to have a local tribesman seconded to me who would be my guide and driver to take me wherever I needed to go. He was almost like a Man Friday and could do almost anything from changing a tyre, cooking an egg on a hot rock or killing and skinning snakes, which were never wasted and made a tasty meal. His talents were endless and he knew the surrounding hills along with their history and geography almost as if he had it all recorded.

Thabo was a proud African tribesman who was quick to smile and liked to please. He said that it was good to travel away from his own village so that he could get some peace away from his five wives and numerous children; he said he could only count up to twelve and didn't know how many children there were. His language was Xhosa but his English was excellent and he chuckled a great deal. I liked him immediately and I had a feeling that he would become a good and trusted friend. He made me feel safe in this vast, wild and beautiful country.

> *Although the origins of the South African Ndebele are shrouded in mystery, they have been identified as one of the Nguni tribes.*
>
> *The Nguni tribes represent nearly two thirds of South Africa's Black population and can be divided into four distinct groups; The Central Nguni (the Zulu speaking peoples), the Southern Nguni (the Xhosa-speaking peoples), the Swazi people from Swaziland and adjacent areas and the Ndebele people of the Northern Province and Mpumalanga*

Thabo, for whatever reason decided to call me Jona-Baas. I didn't encourage it and yet he seemed comfortable using that name. I know Baas was the old Afrikaans word for Boss, and apartheid had now been over for nearly a hundred years, but when I tried to dissuade him he just grinned and said, "OK Jona-Baas."

I discussed my plans with Thabo who listened intently to everything I was telling him although I wasn't sure how much of it he would retain. I soon learnt that he forgot nothing and he would often have solutions and ideas that I hadn't thought of. It was now approaching the end of November and very close to the middle of summer in South Africa. The days were exceedingly hot and sultry and extremely humid; this quickly saps your energy whilst leaving you wringing wet from perspiration.

Our four-wheel drive vehicle did not have any air conditioning and was extremely old, dating back to about 2050. However, it was reliable and seemed to be able to tackle the hardest of terrain. We often managed to get higher into the mountains than I had planned due to its rugged performance, plus Thabo's knowledge of the terrain and the best unmarked routes to take.

The day before our departure from the Kaolin Mine I discussed my plans with my Caltex colleagues on the ground, who were still mapping out some of the areas of great interest for me to look at on my return.

John Hanman had worked for Caltex for over thirty years and had spent most of his time in this location. He must have been in his late sixties with a rugged, dark, almost grizzly appearance, as if he lived entirely in the sun and never went indoors. He was oblivious to the heat and had the capacity to carry on working in the midday sun, even when the temperature was up in the forties. It was always several degrees warmer here than on the coast which was cooled by the offshore breezes that seemed to be prevalent near to the sea.

John's colleague was a young African graduate who had been educated at Caltex's expense in the USA. He had studied for his degree in Geological Sciences at Alabama University and proudly showed me his résumé. It pleased him to make sure that I understood that he was properly educated and not just a local employee. He had a brightly coloured file with all of his university papers and certificates which he carried everywhere with him. On the front of this file in large very legible writing was printed:-

Mission Statement: The Department of Geological Sciences is committed to providing strong educational and research programs that benefit students, the science, society, and the state of Alabama. Our mission is to:

* *Maintain quality educational programs that provide basic geologic instruction to non-majors.*
* *Maintain quality undergraduate programs that prepare students for graduate education or careers in the geological sciences.*
* *Maintain a quality graduate program that provides M.Sc. and Ph.D. students with the skills necessary to carry out independent research and obtain employment in a specialized area of the geological sciences.*
* *Develop and maintain research programs that contribute new knowledge to the geological sciences. Provide service to the scientific community and the public.*
* *Assist in the sound and sustainable economic development of the region, state, and nation.*

He wanted me to know that his ancestors had lived in Alabama way back in 1860 when African Americans made up over forty-five per-cent of the population and he had been privileged to be sent to study for his degree at Alabama University. Back in 1999 his family had finally returned to their native soil in Africa.

They were an unusual pairing but had produced very creditable results as a Ground Survey Team and Caltex praised them highly. They were to be our contact whilst Thabo and I disappeared into the hills. The most important part of our kit was the satellite phones which we tested and checked extensively before packing them safely away in the truck.

By the time it was getting dark Thabo had almost finished packing everything we needed into the truck.

We had discussed the requirements and I didn't need reminding that although it was very hot during the day it would be very cold during the night and the temperature at dusk dropped very quickly in the hills.

Thabo was a real gem and although he looked dishevelled and untidy his brain certainly was not. He had made a list of everything he had packed and knew exactly where it was on the truck. His handwriting and sometimes his spelling were poor and so I have included the list below in English so that you can see how thorough he had been in his preparation.

Equipment

- Rucksack - Kit Bag - Boots
- Gaiters - Sleeping Bag - Roll Mat
- Water Bottles + Flask - Camera + Spare Digital Camera Disks- Sun Glasses + a Spare pair
- Trekking Poles - Bivie Bag
- Mug + Plate + Spoon - Pen Knife / Multi Tool –Lighters + Matches
- Tent - Stove + Fuel Bottle - Pans + Grabber
- Day Shelter - Compass + Maps

Technical

- Head Torch × 2 - Spare Batteries + bulb - Rope
- Helmet - Radio + Batteries - Spare Pick
- Repair Kit (tape, superglue, string, cable ties, strap, needle + thread, pliers)

Clothing

- Waterproof Jacket
- Thermal Top × 2

- Body Warmer - Thick Fleece Trousers
- Thick Socks × 2 - Thin Socks × 2
- Shorts - Casual Trousers + Shirt - Boxers
- Woolly Hat - Mitts × 2
- Gloves × 2
- Sandals - Towel - Sun Hat

Admin.

- Cash
- Business Brief
- Note book + pens/pencils - Books
- Itinerary - Maps + Route descriptions -
- Kit Check Lists - Company Contact Details -Local Agents Details

Wash Bag

- Soap - Tooth brush + Paste - Razors
- Nail Clippers - Moisturiser

Medical

- Wet Wipes - Sun Cream + Lip Cream - First Aid Kit
- Vitamin Tablets

Extra Food / Drink

- Isotonic and or Carbohydrate powdered drinks
- Sweets
- Fruit Tea Bags

This was impressive and I doubt I would have been so thorough. Thabo was grinning like a Cheshire cat and almost childlike as I praised him for his great work. He told me that his wives never gave him any compliments like that even though he had given them all such wonderful beautiful babies.

He said they all took him for granted and he liked to feel appreciated. “Whilst I am away,” he chuckled, “my number one wife will be in charge and she will herd the other wives about like she does the cattle and pigs. When I return they will all smell like the cattle and I will have to take them to the river and bathe them and if they behave maybe I will make some more babies.”

“I need lots of children,” he confided in me, “so that I will have them to take care of me when I am old.”

Several times over the next few weeks I was so grateful that I had Thabo with me. He was always cheerful with a chuckle and a joke but also had a very serious practical side to him and was a great asset and friend. Without him we would not have achieved so many things.

Chapter 7 Into the Hills

Dawn was breaking the following day as Thabo and I set off for the nearby hills. They looked really close but the distance was very misleading because they were in fact over thirty miles away. The early morning sun seemed to shimmer and the hills looked almost close enough to touch.

The going was quite tough; there had been no rain for several weeks and the rough scrub we were driving over was very bumpy and seemed to shake us to our bones with every lurch of the vehicle. I doubt we covered more than 6 miles in the first hour and the distance between us and the hills we were heading for never seemed to change.

The wildlife was extraordinary with a cacophony of sound coming from every direction. I had thought it was going to be quiet out here but far from it. The sounds of crickets, frogs, birds and a myriad of insects and buzzing creatures filled the air. And occasionally there was the sound of something much larger; although I am not sure I wanted to know what they were. We passed quite close to a water hole and there, taking their morning drink, were a couple of buffalo; their strength and size was far greater than I had imagined, they looked enormous and I was grateful that we would not be going too close.

Almost without warning there was a hasty rustling sound coming from a nearby clump; of bushes, we had disturbed the early morning snooze of a rhinoceros. I had never seen one before up close and personal like this, it was truly magnificent, and who would mess with a rhinoceros? Only the grossly foolish, undoubtedly heartless and short-sighted would trouble this noble beast, endowed with great big horns, extremely tough hide, considerable size and a very short fuse. He was certainly grumpy at being disturbed and we took a circuitous route to avoid getting any closer to him.

I was pleased that I had packed extra film for my camera. I had really brought it with me for company purposes not thinking at the time that I might want to be part tourist and take photographs. I did carry a small digital but for close up detail a conventional camera still seems to give better results.

Thabo seemed quite happy to do all of the driving which gave me the chance to enjoy the panoramic scene all around me. Up until now I had thought only of the business and the job at hand but I realised that I could have both in this stunning countryside.

Thabo headed for a clump of trees which he hoped did not have any big cats resting in the shade. We were lucky and he pulled the truck very close to one gnarled old tree so that we could hide away from the hot sun. Elephants had been this way because the bark on the tree was all broken and torn but right now there was no sign of any large animals, either cats or elephants.

We quickly brewed up a cup of hot tea which really is great at quenching the thirst. We also had some hard biscuits that bore a great resemblance to those found in Royal Navy survival kits; thankfully there were no weevils in them.

The truck seemed to be running too hot and we stayed longer than we should have done to let it cool down. When it had cooled enough Thabo filled it with water, he also removed the thermostat which he thought might have been the problem. He says this often happens in this excessive heat and always carried spares. But for now we carried on without one.

It was about mid-afternoon before we reached the foothills and I scoured my maps to make sure that we were still heading for the area that I needed to survey. We needed to adjust our course slightly to the west to get us back on track but we were not far out.

We had a Global Positioning Unit in the truck but out here it was a very hit and miss affair. I don't know whether it is the heat, the mountains or something else but more often than not there was no signal. It always seemed to work better at night so maybe the heat does have something to do with it.

Apart from our earlier tea break we had not eaten and so Thabo set up the cooker and set about preparing a meal. It was not a lavish affair, just a simple stew and some quite fresh bread. We sat in the shadow of the truck and enjoyed our lunch break.

We knew that from here on the route was going to get much harder and I wondered how far we would get before having to proceed on foot. Oh well, time to worry about that when the time came.

I finished my stew and Thabo passed me a cool fruit drink which he told me had a little salt added to replace my body fluids. I had only been in Africa for a few days and was not acclimatised to the humidity and heat and had been sweating profusely since we left Fish Hoek. Thabo chuckled and pointed at me, holding his nose and suggested that I needed a bath; he was right. What I wouldn't have given for a cool dip in the ocean right then.

Away to our right and ambling through a heat haze we saw about seven elephants and couple of babies making their way towards the water hole where we had previously seen the buffalo. It was still quite hot and they were moving very slowly keeping their babies close by. There are too many predators to allow the babies to stroll away from the herd.

If I had thought the first part of the journey was rugged it did not compare with this terrain. Over the next three hours we covered about four miles by which time we needed to start looking for a camp site for the night. We were approaching a hollow in the rocks and it seemed to be a protected area for a camp site. However I was not instantly convinced when Thabo spotted a snake lying in the sun on top of a rock. He said that the snake would soon head away as the sun was setting and it would not enjoy lying on a cold rock. (The thought came to me that we like to lie on the beach when the sun was out and move away when it went in. Not too dissimilar from the snake)

The sun dropped rapidly and as Thabo had said the snake was quickly gone. He soon erected the tents which were of a very modern design and at the pull of a cord they were up. Once again he was chuckling at how easy these tents were compared with the old fashioned ones that used to take him half an hour to put up.

I never felt down whilst this genial fellow was around, always smiling and chuckling. He could make even the worst day seem like an adventure. He said he was looking forward to a good night's rest with no wives or babies to keep him awake. I was also longing for a good night's sleep. I was exhausted and wished I had spent a few more days between leaving England in the middle of winter and being in South Africa in the middle of summer.

The heat and humidity were oppressive although Thabo was cool and relaxed. Before turning in for the night I set up the satellite phone and checked in with John Hanman to see if there had been any instructions or messages. He told me that Brendan had tried to contact me and would I call him whenever it was convenient. I tried to call him but there was no answer and I assumed he was still lecturing because it was still day time in Scotland. It didn't sound as if it was too urgent so I settled down for the night.

I expected to sleep well but the night time was nearly as noisy as the day, except every sound seemed closer and louder. It felt quite spooky and it seemed that all the big cats were sitting at the flap of my tent. I was almost relieved when morning came although I felt completely wrung out. Thabo, of course, seemed to have slept like a baby and was fresh and completely alert. The coffee pot was on the boil and breakfast was well on the way. Whatever it was smelt good, and I was ravenous and ready for some of Thabo's good grub.

It was another hot and humid day, but somehow I did not feel so uncomfortable and was obviously starting to get used to it. As we made our way up the steady incline into the hills I felt relaxed and began thinking that this was what I enjoyed doing. Thabo was happy and singing in a deep melodious voice, although the tune took some getting used to.

As midday approached Thabo started looking for somewhere to stop for a drink and a light lunch. We were only a couple of hours away from our first trig point where we needed to sink our first sonic marker and also take surface samples. I had marked out an area about thirty miles across and various points that I wished to survey. That would be enough to confirm, or otherwise, the viability of sinking a drill in the area. It would also give me enough information as to whether the underground reserves of oil were in fact connected to the oil lake believed to be under the sea.

This whole area was a veritable treasure trove with reserves of so many different commodities: gold, chromium, antimony, coal, iron ore, manganese, nickel, phosphates, tin, uranium, gem diamonds, platinum, copper, vanadium, salt, natural gas and now beneath it all there was a vast reservoir of oil.

Whilst this list of valuable commodities excited the commercial world, how many were interested what the cost would be to the environment and wildlife and of course the local inhabitants who relied on the land for their living?

Here I am now becoming a little self-righteous, and I work for one of the largest and most destructive oil companies in the world. Perhaps, as a geologist, I should be looking at ways to protect the rocks and not destroy them. My musings on the morality of it all lasted only a few moments and then I had my company head back on again.

I told Thabo that we would press on until we reached our first trig point and then we would set up camp.

"Jona-Bass, how long will we stay at camp?" he asked.

"About two days, I think, will be enough to survey this first point and from then on we will probably stop for only one night at each point."

"Ok," he replied, "I will find a good sheltered spot away from the sun and with some protection from any marauding cats."

With that he plunged the truck noisily up an incline covered in small bushes as we forced our way towards the top of nearest hill. It was a hard climb and the truck seemed to scream and complain every inch of the way. There was not much conversation at times like this; for one thing, Thabo was too busy concentrating on keeping the vehicle upright and for the other, the noise of the engine virtually precluded any talking.

By the time we reached our first night's stop on the mountain we were exhausted and several times I had to leave the truck to try and see our way forward and to direct Thabo as best I could. Despite the arduous task, Thabo never once offered any complaint and I was grateful for his reassuring posture.

I must have been getting used to my new environment because I slept soundly and was only disturbed once in the night by the sound of a big cat snarling in the darkness.

Thabo heard me stir and quietly said, “It’s OK, Jona-Baas; cheetah is having his dinner about a mile away.”

When I awoke, breakfast and coffee was already served and it made me wonder if this man ever slept. But despite that he never showed any sign of fatigue or ill temper.

On completion of breakfast I started to remove the kit that I needed for the survey and Thabo asked if he could go and scout around the area. I nodded consent and off he went into the bush carrying a long knife at his waist. He was a strange sight, wearing a pair of scruffy torn off jeans as shorts but he always had on a clean shirt. He had a variety of shirts which he must have acquired from his many friends near Cape Town. The funny part about his shirts was that they all had advertising slogans on them. Coca Cola, Chanel, Christian Dior, Tommy Hilfiger.

When I asked him about them he said, “I only shop in designer shops in London and New York,” and then he ran off chuckling to himself.

I busied myself for the rest of the morning taking samples and readings and filling in my log with all the findings. I also took a lot of photographs of the area and included the chart grid reference on the snaps and a GPS reading. I wanted to make sure everything was right as I had no intention of backtracking because I had made a silly mistake.

At lunchtime Thabo appeared at my side without a sound and he quite startled me. In his left hand he was carrying a red cloth a little larger than a handkerchief from which he produced four fresh eggs and with a beaming grin he brought out his right hand from behind his back in which he held some sort of fowl.

"We will have fresh meat for dinner tonight," he proudly boasted, "and eggs for breakfast. You want them poached or scrambled?"

"Where did you get the red cloth?" I asked him.

"I have friends," he replied with a haughty flourish of his hands.

"What, out here?" I countered.

"I have friends everywhere," he grinned.

By the time I had finished for the day, Thabo had plucked and cleaned the fowl and it was slowly cooking in the roasting pot along with some vegetables that we had brought with us. He then helped me to put all of my equipment away for the night.

The first day had been productive and the results positive and I was feeling rather pleased with the way everything was progressing. However, I was feeling somewhat apprehensive about tomorrow because we would be working only a couple of miles away from the mine which had taken my Uncle and his colleagues all those years ago.

I wanted to go to the top of the mine and pay my respects although I didn't really remember him all that well. I had promised my father that I would and as I was so close, it was the right thing to do. Nevertheless, I had an eerie feeling about it.

Before settling down for the night I tried once more to contact Brendan. Grace answered the phone and, after a couple of minutes of idle chit chat, she passed me over to her father. Brendan informed me that Washington had been in touch and that they appeared to be procrastinating and said that their findings had so far been inconclusive. They also wanted to know exactly where and how they came into my possession.

Neither Brendan nor I liked the way that this was going and I was exceedingly reluctant to give them anything more than they already had. I was now really wishing that I had not been talked into letting them go.

"I have already told them that you are working in South Africa and are completely out of touch. I will just tell them that they will have to wait for your return, which could be several months away. That will at least give you time to come up with an answer."

"Is there any possibility that we can ask for the samples to be returned?" I asked him.

"I could try," he said, "but you know what these Washington types are like, they are not likely to give you anything back."

We chatted idly for a few minutes but he had to go as he had promised Grace that he would take her out for dinner.

The following morning it was overcast and quite a bit cooler. I didn't mind at all and it was quite a relief not to feel quite so sticky. As we broke camp it started to drizzle and for a few minutes I let it cool me down. However, I quickly realised that this was not going to be good.

The going was hard enough but now with the ground wet, the truck had difficulty with the grip and slid around frequently. Nevertheless we plunged forward and upwards and within a couple of hours were on the top of a very large plateau. From here we could see almost the whole area that I intended to survey.

It was only a couple of miles to our next point and now that we were on the top of the plateau we made much better time. I was soon offloading the equipment for my next check. Whilst I set up the gear Thabo made a brew of hot tea. It was a lot cooler now and in contrast to the past few days the tea had a warming effect.

A couple of times, whilst taking the soundings, I had the strange idea that we were being watched. At first I ignored it, but although I hadn't seen anyone, the feeling became stronger.

"Thabo, are we alone up here?" I asked him.

"No, Jona-Baas, there are hunters in the area," he replied.

"I hope it's not us they are hunting," I said, jokingly.

"Not us, just small deer for their meal pot," he said.

Apparently the small hill deer are very tasty and a popular meal for the local tribes people.

Thabo told me a little about his tribal friends. They were a small group known as the Nama. The Nama originally lived around the Orange River in southern Namibia and northern South Africa. Before this the Nama lived in Namaqualand and were called Hottentots. They are thought to be the true descendants of the Khoikhoi. Today there are very few of them left.

Unfortunately they came into conflict with the Herero who were already in this area, and the groups fought many wars. They were now living in this jungle area close to the Cape.

Chapter 8 Finding the Mine

I completed my latest work quite quickly because I was aware that I wanted to try and visit the caved-in mine and my Uncle's last resting place. It was much closer than I had anticipated and within about only thirty minutes we could see the metal poles that marked the entrance to the old mine. The metal poles and the sheets of metal covering the entrance were very rusty and were overgrown with bushes and lush green grasses and weeds.

There was a plaque marking the spot but even that was covered in verdigris and barely legible. I tried to rub off some of the green but could only make out the letters 'arl', and a 'Pa Dr', and 'Bai', and finally and lot clearer, was the name Peter Hawkes.

It would be guessing to say that maybe the 'a r l' were part of Carl but I had no clue what the rest were as I had no idea at this time of the names of the others, apart from one whose name was still clear. Still, I took some photographs which I thought my father might like to see.

The only history I had of the mine and the accident was from a newspaper cutting that I had folded and carried in my wallet.

CAPE TOWN, South Africa – On 12th May, 1995, a twelve ton underground locomotive and an elevator cage filled with miners crashed to the bottom of the No. 2 shaft at Moore's Gold Mine. Recovery teams brought up the first few bodies of what may be possibly more than 100 dead.

The only confirmation reaching the surface was that there were no survivors.

How the locomotive - used on the 56 level, 1,700 metres down - plunged into the shaft is not known. It appears to have tipped into the shaft as the cage containing night-shift miners was on its way up from the lower levels. The locomotive crashed into the elevator cage 500 metres from the bottom of the shaft, snapping the cable and sending the cage plummeting down. Sabotage was strongly suspected but the mine was closed down and sealed at the surface.

The following is a note that I added to the News cutting.

'In 2072 nearly 80 years later a small team led by my Uncle, Carl Jonesy, opened up the cap on top of the mine to begin an investigation into what might have happened all those years before and also to see if there was any viability in reopening the shaft. It was only day 4 of the survey when Uncle Carl and his 2 colleagues and a local guide met with a mishap at about 1,000 feet down the mine and a rock fall put an end to the survey and all future plans to investigate was curtailed permanently. None of the bodies were ever recovered.'

Chapter 9
The Warriors' Ceremony

As I searched around the top of the mine there were breaks in the foliage as if someone or something, maybe an animal, had disturbed it. I then found a small entrance, not big enough, I thought for a man so presumed that it must have been an animal. Once more I had this feeling that we were being watched. I looked round for Thabo but he had disappeared.

"Thabo," I called, "where are you?"

A few minutes later he appeared and just behind him was a young local warrior. He stopped a good way off and would not come any closer. Thabo came forward to speak to me. He was very excited.

"Jona-Baas, there have been people here before, not long ago in the mine."

"What do you mean in the mine?"

"My friend says that many people came from a strange tribe and some of the children went into the mine."

"Can I talk to your friend?" I asked him.

"No, he says it is not allowed."

I think he was trying to tell me that it was bad medicine but he could not find the right words.

I asked Thabo to go and talk to his new friend and see what he could find out.

A while later he came back and said, "My friend has invited me to the village to go and eat with them and talk to the old men. He says that they will be able to tell me more about these strange people."

After Thabo had left me I took a good look around the area to see if I could find out anything else. I found nothing unusual and went back to the camp and set about having some supper. I didn't know when Thabo would return but I had no intention of going hungry while I waited for him. It was just as well because he did not return until dawn the following day. He came back into camp singing a happy song and looking very pleased with himself.

"I think I have another Wife," he grinned.

"I don't think I want to know," I told him. "So what did the old men tell you?" I urged.

Thabo kept moving away from the story to talk about his new found love and I had to keep bringing him back to finding out what I needed to know.

Eventually I managed to get some details out of him and it took him a long time to tell his story. However I managed to glean the following information;

There is a tribe of people who are called the Himba; they are semi nomadic pastoralists who until a few years ago lived in Kaokoland, which is about 1,000 miles to the north-west. They live by herding sheep, goats and some cattle and they frequently move about so they can graze their livestock.

The Himba believe in ancestor worship and rituals concerning sacred fire (okoruwo) which they say are an important link between the living and the dead.

They are striking people to look at and the Himba women go topless and wear mini-skirts made of goat skins adorned with shells and jewellery made of iron and copper. The men wear goatskin loincloths.

They have long tried to keep themselves isolated from the rest of the world and over a period of many years they have moved slowly south east in the direction of Cape Town to avoid contact with civilisation. Whenever they do come into contact with other humans they will only communicate through local tribes people.

Thabo said that they have now settled on the pasture slopes on the far side of the plateau. I asked Thabo how we could ask them about the mine and why they were interested in it. He said he would talk to his friends and see how this could be accomplished.

Thabo was keen to go and talk to the old men and to find out as much as he could about communicating with the Himba. I had the feeling that his interest in talking to the 'old men' was far more personal than my needs but was more about his latest conquest.

What followed next was a very lengthy process. The local leader of the tribe would have to go and meet the Himba leader and arrange a contest. For all negotiations there had to be ceremony of building friendship. This would take the form of about five pre-pubescent boys in combat with similar boys from the Himba. They had to prove their manhood and the chance to earn the hand of a chosen virgin. Several virgins from each tribe would be selected from their eligible girls. They would then be kept closeted in a separate area and would spend several days with older married sisters who would pamper them and prepare them.

This beautifying process included bathing in goat's milk, brushing and combing the hair, dying it with a type of henna and tying it into braids. The lower half of the body was painted with a body dye and finally jewellery would adorn every other part of the body. Heavy necklaces, ear rings, finger rings, toe rings and face paint. Each one was similar but totally unique and no girl looked the same.

On the day of the ceremony all other women would have their heads shaved. No one was allowed to look more beautiful than these maidens. On the special day the girls would all be seated around a large arena. They would be totally naked but their charms would be hidden by the lower body paint and the length of the necklaces that adorned their necks.

The young, would be warriors would have all their body hair removed and they would be covered from head to toe with red ochre, (iron oxide mixed with clay) and they would wear short loin cloths made of leather strips. On the night of the ceremony each boy from each tribe would be given an implement with which he had to fight. 1) A wooden paddle, 2) a leather multi-thonged whip, 3), a crude looking cudgel, 4) a wooden staff, 5), no weapon at all. For the first fight the boys would face each other, one couple at a time carrying the same weapon.

The winner of each bout would advance into the second and subsequent rounds. After the first round each winner could choose the weapon of his choice. The winner of each bout would be the contestant who either rendered his opponent unconscious or removed him from the ring.

On completion of the ceremony the overall winner would be allowed to select the maiden of his choice and this might be from his own tribe or that of the other tribe. More often than not they would choose from the other tribe because this was the way to create peace between two tribes. There were no losers on the night so provided a warrior was conscious then he would be allowed to choose a girl as his woman.

This whole process was just so that the elders of the local tribe could converse with the Himba and ask any questions. Once the ceremony was complete then both sides were honour bound to talk to each other and to tell the truth. Sadly, as a complete outsider I was not allowed to attend or to talk to any of the elders on either side. I had to rely on Thabo conveying my questions to the local elders so that they could ask their Himba counterparts.

It was a stressful time and I was also concerned about the time all this would take and how much time I dared to be away in the hills before the people at Caltex started to question my absence.

I didn't see a lot of Thabo over the next few days and all I could get out of him was, "But, Jona-Baas, I have much work to do if you want all the answers."

I knew what his motives were but what could I say. I couldn't complain. After all, whilst we were working he always did the work of two people.

I had briefed him fully on questions that I needed answers to. More than anything, I needed to know why the Himba children had gone into the sealed mine and also what they had found. There were many other minor questions but these were the main two.

I spent most those few days whilst Thabo was away completing as many of the surveys as I could. Getting from one point to the next was not too difficult as the terrain around the rim of the plateau was gently undulating and quite easy to negotiate in the truck. I think I missed him most at meal times because after a fairly strenuous day unloading my gear and then loading it up again I was not in a mood for cooking. Eggs were easy to come by and so my main diet was eggs and they only took a few minutes to prepare.

On the day of the great ceremony I returned to our main camp of the first day on the mountain and close to the closed mine. I know I could not attend but I wanted to be close by. I wondered if I might hear any of the activities from my vantage point above the village. I did not have to wait very long before I heard the sound of the Himba women ululating on their way to the event. I had always thought that they only made that screeching noise at funerals but it is apparently a celebratory call as well.

(ULULATING is a long, wavering, high-pitched sound resembling the howl of a dog or wolf with a trilling quality. It is produced by emitting a high pitched loud noise accompanied with a rapid movement of the tongue and the uvula. The term ululation is an onomatopoeic word derived from Latin. It is produced by moving the tongue, rapidly, from left to right repetitively in the mouth while producing a sharp sound).

I had no idea how long it took for a ceremony like this but I knew I was in for a long wait. I could hear the noise resounding up the valley towards me and as the day progressed it seemed to get louder and louder. Every now and then I could hear girls squealing and the unmistakable sound of African singing voices wafted in on the breeze being accompanied by a very rhythmic sound of drums. I lay under my canvas tent listening to the partying going on below me and I don't know when it ended because I must have fallen asleep.

When I awoke it was pitch black and was very late into the night. I wondered what had caused me to stir from such a deep sleep. And then I heard a scraping noise just beyond the tent flaps. I crawled quietly and gently forward so that I could peer out of the tent and see what had disturbed me. Not nine or ten feet from the tent were two young leopards. I was highly surprised to see them and was immediately cautious because where there are cubs there is usually an unpredictable mother. The cubs scampered over to my makeshift food store and within seconds had discovered the two eggs I had planned to have for the following morning's breakfast.

I was fascinated with the way they played for several minutes with the eggs without breaking them. They soon became bored with that game and the eggs were quickly broken and devoured. Then they disappeared into the back of the truck and I wondered how much damage they could do in there. Fortunately I did not have to wait very long before I heard an urgent roar from nearby. Mother was looking for them and they quickly scampered in the direction of their anxious mother.

That was my action for the evening and I settled down again and was soon asleep. I had many dreams that night; there were lions in the camp and elephants and dark warriors and all of them hell bent on ending my useless life. Half naked girls and angry snakes and a constant feeling of falling down a cold, eerie damp mine shaft.

I was relieved when daylight woke me from my demons. Thabo had returned. I was so pleased to see him and there he was cooking my breakfast as if it was just another normal day.

"Where are the eggs Jona-Baas?" he called as he heard me stumbling around in my tent.

"Cats had them," I shouted back. "Not that you care."

"Oh, you had visitors," he laughed.

“I could have been eaten in my bed,” I shouted back at him.

“I don’t think so, you are much too salty for their taste,” he retorted.

I was almost too nervous to ask him about the exciting events of the night before. But I did not have to wait long before he started to tell me. So many beautiful girls and fearless warriors, too much liquor and food and dancing, it was magnificent he said animatedly. He was full of it and spent the next hour telling me in detail about the fights and the dancing and the tantalising Himba girls. I laughed at him and told him he had enough wives and he replied, quite seriously, “I have room for more.”

I sat quietly and had my breakfast, dying to ask him more serious questions. When I finally got to the point he just brushed it off as not important and left me in a slough of total despair.

I was beginning to wonder if any of my questions had been posed to or answered by the Himba. Thabo seemed preoccupied and said that he needed time to think. When I finally managed to get him to talk he was nervous and fidgety.

“I am angry and feel insulted, Jona-Bass, they wouldn’t let me talk to the Himba elders, and I had thought them my friends.”

When all the singing and dancing and celebrations were complete and the young warriors had gone off with their chosen woman, only then did the elders sit down and talk. There were 4 elders from each side but Thabo was told to go and wait with his woman whilst they talked. He didn’t go but sat behind a tree just a few yards away. Sadly, he could not hear the conversation and had very little to offer in the way of answers. They sat and talked for many hours and every now and then some of the womenfolk would take in hot food and refreshments.

When the conference was over, several of the women returned to the elders with cauldrons of hot water and bathed their feet. It seemed to be a local tradition that Thabo said did not happen in his tribe. They then dried the Nama elders' feet and the Himba elders stood up and bowed deeply to their hosts and then disappeared into the jungle.

I was frustrated and almost shouted at Thabo, "What happened at the mine and what did the children find?"

Thabo looked unhappy and hung his head in shame and disappointment. "I don't know, Jona-Baas, I don't know."

I couldn't just leave it like that without any answers but right then I was tired and didn't know how to proceed from there. Thabo was hurting and felt that he had been humiliated. He wandered over to his tent and disappeared inside and remained in there for the rest of the day and that night. I left him there and climbed up to the mine entrance wondering if there might be any clues that I had missed.

There was nothing else to see and I returned to the camp as darkness fell. I brewed up a cup of tea and sat down outside my tent to contemplate what to do next. Finally I gave up and went into my tent and settled into my sleeping bag. I was deeply troubled but still managed to sleep quite soundly and did not stir until nearly ten o'clock next morning.

Thabo seemed to have forgotten his doldrums and was whistling cheerfully as he handed me some hot coffee. We also had eggs for breakfast and I wondered where he had managed to get them from as the young leopards had eaten what we had left the previously

The weather had changed again and it was a bright and sunny morning although the clouds in my mind still hung heavy and I was wondering what to do. I did not have long to wait because before I had finished breakfast, Thabo suddenly jumped to his feet and said, “They are summoning me, I must go.”

“Go where?” I asked him.

Two young Nama warriors suddenly materialised about twenty yards away to the east of the camp, waving their spears and beckoning Thabo. With a quick smile he scampered off towards them.

He was back within about two hours and came into the camp with a huge grin on his face and looking very pleased with himself.

“I have them,” he chuckled, as he fidgeted and jumped up and down.

“What do you have?” I asked him. By now even I was smiling because his mood was so infectious.

“I have the answers,” he cried.

Thabo needed to compose himself and I remembered how frustrated I had been the night before and so did not want to hurt his feelings any more. He strolled over to the cooker and put a pan of water on to boil. He quickly made us both a cup of tea and then came and sat cross legged in front of me.

“Jona,” he started, this time omitting the Baas, “There is much to tell.”

I made him wait whilst I got a pad and pencil as I wanted to document everything that he was going to tell me.

Chapter 10 The Himba

Thabo then began his story of what had been relayed to him by the Nama elders.

The Himba had only arrived in this area about six years previously and spent a great deal of time exploring the area before deciding to settle. They were aware of the other tribe but rarely came into contact and when they did both sides politely kept their distance. After all, there was enough room out there for both tribes as long as neither looked for trouble or tried to take liberties territorially. There was an unspoken line drawn between the two and this was always respected.

The Himba had settled to the north west of the plateau where there was plenty of grazing land for their animals and they often explored the plateau and picked berries and fruit which grew in abundance on these slopes.

At some stage during their early days here they came across the capped mine. They knew nothing of its history or why it was closed but they did know that the bright gold metal that came from such places was very valuable to those who lived in the big cities. At first they could not gain entrance because the top had been capped with metal and concrete and just below the surface dynamite had been used to block the shaft. They eventually found a way in but it was too small for any of the grown men to gain access. Several young boys had gone in but did not like it because it was too dark and they knew there was a deep hole going down a long way.

Near the top of the shaft were a number of small passageways, some of which went downwards for several metres, but not to any great depth. They explored these passageways and eventually found several more much larger entrances hidden in the undergrowth around the plateau. These had all been dug out by hand and it seemed fairly obvious that they were intended as vent holes to allow the mine as much ventilation as possible.

Of course with the discovery of the larger vent holes, fully grown men could now gain access to the mine. Apart from the thought of the gold, the Himba are very inquisitive people and wanted to explore this underground world. Their biggest problem was not climbing down into the ground but how they could see once they were in there.

At first their progress had been slow and they had to attach wooden stakes to the side of the shaft wrapped with cloth that had been dipped in animal fat and then ignited. Inch by inch they ventured further down the shaft using a wicker basket, made by the women, to lower themselves slowly down.

They made a break through which made their progress a lot quicker, easier and safer. At about fifty feet down the shaft opened up into a very large cavern that looked as if half of it was a natural cave and the rest had been hewn out by man.

Along the walls of the cavern were about twenty locked cages and the contents could be clearly seen from the outside. There were boots, helmets, torches, oil lamps, coats, as well as a number of private things, letters, knives, flasks, photographs, pens, pencils and even mobile phones. The Himba did not know what the mobile phones were but Thabo managed to explain in quite good detail what they looked like. Thabo had seen many mobile phones so guessed immediately what they were.

At the end of this row of cages was a large metal enclosed store and inside they found hundreds of torch batteries, wrapped in waterproof boxes, oil lanterns and at the back of the store was a tank containing oil for the lanterns. There were also a couple of diving suits, masks, flippers, oxygen tanks, knives and coils of rope. To the Himba this was a real treasure trove, although they had no idea what the diving suits and all the other associated equipment was.

Although they are a very inquisitive race of people and enjoy owning trinkets of every description, they never made any attempt to remove any of the items from the mine. They were quite happy to use the equipment in the mine but they would never take it away. They were very superstitious and did not wish to incur the wrath of the ancestors of the mine people. They still strongly believe in a strong link between them and the dead as part of their religion.

They had no way of knowing how long ago the mine had been abandoned or even why but they were surprised at the condition of everything that they found. All the lockers were tidy, the floors were clean and there seemed very little dust or excess dirt anywhere in the mine. Even the lamps and all the equipment looked as if it had recently been cleaned. As if it was all waiting for their owners to reclaim them.

The first few attempts at descending to the bottom of the mine had been thwarted by the incredible depth of the shaft. They had no way of knowing how far it was to the bottom. Unfortunately the ropes that they had were only about 250 feet long. After a series of attempts they found out that there were many levels to the shaft and often many of these levels disappeared a mile or more into the hillside.

At each level they found more and more equipment and after some time accumulated hundreds of metres of rope. They had already ascertained that it was a long way down and they formulated a plan of how they could achieve it. They decided to bring food down into the mine stopping off as they went to make a store. In each store they put ropes, food, lamps and a lowering basket. The women of the tribe were put to work making as many baskets as they could. This whole process took over two years to complete. When it was done they had supplies and equipment lodged at every 200 feet down to a level of about 4,000 feet, not realising that even when they reached their target they were still less than halfway down.

They spent many months in the shaft descending as far as they could. They were hugely disappointed when it dawned on them that they did not have the technology to plumb the depths of this shaft. At last they admitted defeat and slowly and dejectedly returned to the surface, and on the way returned most of the equipment they had taken with them.

They decided not to bring up the ropes thinking that at some time in the future they might wish to return and make another attempt.

It had taken Thabo most of the day to relate this story and for me to document everything he told me. Many times I had to go back over some of the minor details to make sure that I had written it all correctly. We had a break and Thabo cooked an evening meal.

Suddenly after our meal he jumped up and said, "I am so sorry, Jona-Baas, there is something I forgot to tell you."

"What did you forget Thabo?" I asked.

"I forgot to tell you that the Himba went back to the mine again later," he said.

"Well much later the Himba went into the mine again but only descended to about five levels, about a thousand feet and found that the stuff they had left behind had been disturbed and some of it was missing completely. Many of the ropes were gone as were oil and oil lamps and whoever had been there had swept the floor before leaving because there were brush signs on the floor and even one or two twigs which had fallen out of the broom that they used. Because of their beliefs in the dead they believed that it was the dead who had done the work down there."

"Well Thabo, I don't believe in the living dead and whoever had done this was certainly of living flesh and blood. They can believe what they like."

Still despite their beliefs or mine it was certainly very curious. I was disappointed with the end result but it left a burning desire within me to get to the bottom of it all, and I smiled ruefully as I realised my pun.

The Caltex survey needed to be completed and I was not in a position to spend any more time trying to find answers. However the area was so remote that it would be unlikely for anyone apart from the Himba to go snooping around. It would have to wait for another day.

Thabo and I spent the next week completing the work on and around the plateau and I prepared my field study and results ready for presentation on our return. It was a job well done and the results proved without doubt that there was a substantial amount of oil waiting to be released from its subterranean confines.

Somehow in my report I gave the impression that the best option would be to drill out in the open ocean as it would be a much simpler operation. There was, however, a personal reason, and that was that I did not want the area around the mine disturbed by the huge machinery of Caltex. I wanted to leave it undisturbed until I could get the chance to descend into the dark depths of the mine and discover its secrets.

We were soon back at the old Kaolin Mine near Fish Hoek and my two Caltex colleagues were there to meet me. I mentioned nothing of the mine or anything that was not related to the survey. Thabo would certainly not tell anyone as he had made some very special friends during our field trip and he was not about to share them with anyone. So we both had our secrets and for that I was grateful.

John, Madoda and I spent the next couple of days combining the results that we had achieved. Both of them concurred that the best suggestion would be an ocean platform.

I am not sure if I convinced them or whether we really did think it was the right way to go. I couldn't help feeling that I had done my share of pushing in that direction. With the report completed I said my farewells to the team and Thabo took me by Land Rover back to Cape Town.

I spent a couple of days unwinding at a small clean hotel and then booked myself on a flight back to Aberdeen and the corporate offices of Caltex.

Thabo was keen to get back to his wives and horde of children and I was quite sad to see him go. I told him that I would return one day to go back and visit the mine. He made me promise that I would include him in my future plans in South Africa, whatever they were. For the second time he called me Jona.

"Hamba kahuhle" (Xhosa meaning, goodbye-stay well) and then in English,

"Return soon, Jona mhlobo." (friend)

I called Brendan before getting on my flight back to London. I was unable to get a direct flight into Aberdeen and so I had to fly back to London Heathrow. I never enjoyed flying into London; it was always so busy and after a long flight the last thing I wanted was the hustle, bustle of one of the busiest airports in the world. I would get the overnight train to Aberdeen and Brendan offered to pick me up from the station.

Chapter 11 A Threat from Washington and a Plan

I tried to sleep on the flight but only managed to doze off occasionally. My mind was far too busy trying to cope with all the things that had happened in the last few weeks. I still had samples that I need to attend to and Washington was apparently getting quite agitated at my absence. I had wished that I could have returned to Aberdeen and have time to relax for a few days but the way things were gearing up I doubted whether I would get the opportunity.

I half dreamed about a week's holiday in the Canary Islands where I could unwind in the gentle sun and enjoy some swimming and maybe a little sailing. That was all it was, just a dream.

Heathrow airport was as I expected, total chaos with people moving in all directions and pushing trolleys at break neck speeds. I managed to get through customs and immigration quite quickly but then there was the long tedious wait for the baggage to be unloaded from the plane and brought down to the carousel. The arrival of my cases was incredibly slow and the Baggage Handlers go slow action did not help. They were on a go slow wanting more money, didn't everybody? I eventually extricated my cases from the carousel and made my way to the tube station.

Although it was incredibly busy, the tubes ran very quickly and I was soon on my way to King's Cross Station. I then had to lug my bags from there for about ten minutes to get to Euston Station. I was quite lucky and there was room on the Caledonian Sleeper which would take me direct to Aberdeen. There were several stops on the way but I wouldn't have to change trains, I might even get good night's sleep. The sleeper leaves Euston at 21.15 arriving in Aberdeen at 07.35 the following morning.

I had dinner on the train but it was a quick affair as all I really wanted to do was get to some sleep. I indulged in a large cognac before retiring for the night, but hey, Caltex was footing the bill. Before turning in I remembered to take out an extra t-shirt and thick pullover. The east coast of Scotland was very cold at that time of year and the last thing I needed was pneumonia.

It may seem a strange thing to say but I seemed to have lost all track of time whilst I was away and the contrast between the autumn in the North Atlantic, high summer in South Africa and back to the winter in Scotland was quite numbing. As I dozed off to sleep to the rhythmic sound of the train on the rails I realised that the day after tomorrow would be Christmas Eve and I was dumping myself on the kindness of Brendan and Grace.

Brendan was at the station the following morning and was delighted to see me. Grace had remained at home and was preparing the spare bedroom for me to occupy. Whilst we were driving to Brendan's home I borrowed his mobile phone and called Caltex. As it was so close to Christmas, I had no idea when they wished to see me. I was invited to come to the office on December 28th and to bring all my survey results and notes with me.

Brendan quickly brought up the subject of the samples that had been sent to Washington. Apparently they had been in constant touch wanting to know when I would return to the UK. I told him that we needed to discuss the results and I would give them a call after Christmas.

"What exactly is the problem with the results?" I asked Brendan.

"It seems that they are having difficulty in identifying the substances and need to know a lot more about them. Give it a break and enjoy a few days off, Petrey, before you start worrying about Washington scientists. Anyway Grace is really looking forward to seeing you. She is on school holidays until 6th January."

Christmas was great time and Brendan and Grace certainly looked after me and kept me entertained. It was good to totally relax.

I chatted to Mum and Dad on the phone on Christmas morning. Things were looking up; they had gone to spend Christmas at an archaeological dig in the Holy Land. And there was me thinking that they would never do anything exciting. They were having fun and really enjoying it.

Grace was now turned seventeen and was still very keen to go to university to study geology but she was fascinated with criminology and said she would like to study forensic geology. I encouraged her and I somehow knew that she would love it and enjoy it as well.

She had already investigated universities that could offer a Forensic Geology course and had made enquiries more deeply into what she would need to be accepted at Birdbeck University of London.

I had a long talk with Brendan about what had happened out in South Africa and we discussed going out there to resolve the mystery of the mine. I told him that I would like to spend a lot more time doing just that but my career and earning a living was getting in the way.

"You know, Petrey, there may be a way that it could be done but it would take some time to set it up."

"What do you have in mind, Brendan?"

He pondered the question for a few minutes before giving me an answer.

"Well there are three sources of finance for a project like this and we could get a little from each one if we can prove our case. The only thing is that it may take up to two years to put this all together. Do you want me to put wheels in motion and see what I can do?"

We discussed late into the night what we would need for such a complex plan and started making up several lists of requirements.

1. Funding
2. Colleagues to take with us
3. Help on the ground, Thabo etc.
4. Equipment
5. Help with travel

The three main sources of funding options we had were:

1. University
2. Government
3. Commercial

However commercial might give us several and joint options and Brendan said he would start on that angle immediately.

I felt a bit of a fraud leaving him to do all the work but I was still required by Caltex to earn my keep. He drew up a list of possible high profile companies, which he split into two further categories.

1. Cash funding
2 Travel sponsorship.

Anyway I had a date with the board of directors for Caltex and left Brendan to his lists and funding. I think he considered it was his mid-life crisis and he needed this sort of challenge. I, on the other hand, had too much going on, and anyway I was too young for a mid-life crisis.

At 08.45 on 28th January 2086 I presented myself to the Board of Directors of Caltex. I felt somewhat outnumbered as there were seventeen faces sitting round the boardroom table, all very keen to hear about the oilfield in South Africa.

I laid out my carefully prepared charts and figures and gave them a full presentation, being careful not to mention anything about the Gold Mine. I needed to keep them completely in the dark about that. Fortunately they were of the same opinion that the deep water route would be the best. It was now out of my hands and now down to the CEO and the politicians to do their work.

Several of the Directors patted me on the back and said all the right words, and then we were all off to the Park Inn in Aberdeen town centre. What a dreary looking building. From the outside it looked like a tired office block. However, once inside it was plush and inviting and I have to say, the food was magnificent.

After lunch we retired to the lounge where I was given extra special treatment and offered copious amounts of expensive

Cognac. I wondered why they were giving me the Royal treatment. After the drinks, the CEO, Charles Harker, invited us all into one of the hotel's conference rooms which had already been prepared in advance.

Charles started the proceedings by telling everyone that he was very proud of our successes in the past twelve months and that there was much to look forward to over the coming months particularly after the successful in depth work done in South Africa.

He talked about bonuses and pay increments about which everyone was interested. There were also special payments made to various members and I suddenly found myself at the front of the room shaking hands with the CEO and receiving a cheque for £15,000. I was quite shaken up at the generous gesture. I soon realised that it wasn't just for past glories but for softening me up for the next project.

At the end of the meeting everyone drifted away but Charles came and touched my shoulder and asked me to hang on for a few minutes. Finally there was only Charles, Peter Fenneck, Operations Director, and Stephen Pensell, Managing Director of Middle and Far East Operations.

Charles started off by saying, "Well done, Petrey, you have done a grand job and we can see you are capable of great things. How old are you, about thirty? You have done exceedingly well to get this far in such a short period of time and we would like to make that work and effort worthwhile."

"What do you have in mind, Sir?" I asked him.

He started off on a long speech about politics and borders and being able to negotiate with our partners and our enemies etc. etc. I was beginning to wonder where this was leading when it suddenly came to an abrupt end.

"We would like to promote you as our Special Project Director for a sensitive collaboration between Caltex and IOC (Indian Oil Company) they are the largest commercial oil company owning more than fifty per cent of all Indian Oil based in Sadiq Nagar, New Delhi."

Charles was an old school tie sort of guy and clasped his arm around my shoulder and said, "Well what do you think of that, my boy," he beamed at me and the other two men.

"Thank you," I said wondering what I had got myself into.

We all made our way back to the corporate offices where I was to be given a brief on the forthcoming project. I was aware that before I left the UK for another foreign project I needed to call Washington and also James Durbin. James, I imagined was still waiting for my results on the samples that he had given me, although there was still little to tell at this stage.

I took advantage of being in the office to contact Emio Swarzkof in Washington. I dug the phone number out of my wallet and made the call. I knew that we were several hours ahead in the UK but assessed that it must be after 10am in Washington. Nevertheless, Emio had not turned up to the office yet and so I asked the receptionist to be sure to tell him that I had called. I gave her the phone number of Caltex switchboard and told the girl that I would be in the office until about 6pm local time.

The plan in India was a JV (Joint Venture) with IOC. Caltex was going to invest a great deal of money, not only to share in the proceeds of the oil but also to get a foothold into the Indian sub-continent which would be invaluable in the coming years.

In Asia it is very much about whom you know and what mutual benefit you can give to each other. I will not go so far as to say that it is corrupt but you get the idea. At this point I was not feeling very enthusiastic about India as my thoughts were still on the unfinished business I had in South Africa. What I didn't realise right then was that going to India would be one of the best decisions I ever made and one with huge consequences.

I stayed a lot later at the office than I intended but that was quite fortunate because a call came through for me from Emio in Washington. Are all Americans this friendly, I thought to myself as Emio tried his best to make me believe I was a great guy and really very special. I quickly realised that it was a softening up process. I had already been the recipient of some of that process earlier today by the CEO, oh yes, I thought, another American

"About these samples?" he started. "Where did you say they came from?"

"I didn't," I replied.

"Yes, of course, so where did they come from?" he tried again.

I was not in a hurry to give too much away and countered with,

"Why, what makes them so interesting?"

"Well," he said after a few seconds silence. "There is only one or two places in the world that these samples could have come from and those sources are very confidential."

"Really?" I responded. "Then so is the location that they were found."

"Oh come on, Petrey. Can I call you Petrey?"

This guy was starting to get under my skin and I was starting to get agitated.

"Just return the samples and we will forget all about it," I postured.

"Petrey, we can't do that and I really do need to know their origin."

We had reached a stalemate with neither side wanting to give in. I felt that I had no more to say on the matter and told him that I had important things to do and perhaps he would be kind enough to send me all the details that he had to date in a letter, and gave him Brendan's address.

"Goodbye for now, Petrey, you know of course that this is not the end, we will be in touch."

There was a hint of menace in the way that he said *'will'*. What a bizarre call, I thought to myself as I put down the receiver.

I made a call to James Durbin on the Extra. They were back at sea, plodding up and down the same stretch of water but there had been no further strange incidents. I asked James if he had divulged any of the information to anyone else; he said not. I told him there was something strange about the way Washington was dealing with samples and of Emio's veiled threat. I told him briefly of my trip to Africa and my impending departure to India. He asked me to keep him informed of any developments with regards the samples.

Just as a parting gesture he said that he was due to finish his time in the Royal Navy within a year and if I had any suitable jobs, he would be interested. I ended the call thinking to myself that he was a good man in the event of a crisis and a hard worker too. I also enjoyed his company socially even though there were many years difference in our ages.

Chapter 12
New Challenges in India

I still wasn't used to this fast commercial world that I was now part of but it seemed I was destined to spend my future flying from one destination to another. It felt like only yesterday that I was at Heathrow Airport and here I was back at Terminal 4 sitting in the Business Lounge waiting for my flight to New Delhi.

The lounge was comfortable and I wanted a glass of red wine, however, there was very little on offer at the bar apart from Johnny Walker Whisky. I do not like whisky and settled for a soft drink. Once on board the situation was similar and it appears that Indian Airlines only really cater for Indians, who of course love Scotch whisky.

It was an overnight flight, taking about 11 hours to reach our destination. The on board meal was not haute cuisine but it was passable and after eating I settled down to try and sleep. I was very restless and could not get used to sleeping on a plane.

I must have slept eventually because the next thing I was aware of was the cabin lights coming on and the stewardess offering fruit juice or water. Breakfast followed swiftly and the

Captain announced that we would be landing in Delhi in fifty minutes, about half an hour ahead of schedule.

As I stepped out of the airport at Delhi I was almost overcome by the incredible heat, even though it was about 6am. It was about 40 degrees Celsius and it seemed to suck the air out of your lungs and breathing in was quite painful. I hope I can get used to this, I thought.

A man in a suit carrying a name board with my name on it was waving it about like a madman. What was he doing wearing a suit in this heat? I walked over to him and introduced myself.

"I am Chandrasiri," he smiled. "Come."

We were soon, thankfully, in an air conditioned car and out into the crazy traffic of Delhi. The deafening sound of car horns filled the air and it seemed as if everyone with a car just had to make as much noise as possible. I couldn't see the point because everyone else just ignored it.

I was also overcome by the strong smells that invaded my head as we inched our way through the early traffic. It was a smell of rubber, curry, herbs and carbon emissions all rolled into one overpowering aroma. I hated it but that would change into one of recognition and even pleasure on repeat trips to India.

Chandrasiri described himself as the Senior Company Courier, a posh name for a company driver, who talked incessantly and never seemed to need a reply to anything he said. His English, I have to say, was impeccable and he was delighted when I told him so.

We soon arrived at our destination and a huge sign hung over the impressive doors of an old colonial building with the words Asia Petrochemical Company and IOC. The outside may have been old colonial but the interior was far from it. The inside had been torn out and replaced with the most modern, air conditioned offices that you could imagine, with smart well-dressed men and women scurrying to and fro or sat at computer desks.

I felt like Doctor Livingstone in Africa as a loud voice boomed, “Peter Jonesy, I presume.”

“Hello,” I replied, “actually it’s Petrey”

“OK Petrey, I’m Ronald Gomez, welcome to India, is this your first visit?”

“Yes,” I replied.

“I know you have had a long flight so I will whisk you round the office to say hello to everyone, and then get you to your hotel for you to settle in.”

The next few days were all hustle and bustle as I was taken round to visit every department. I met so many people and would not remember who they were and many of them I would probably never see again. My main task here would be out in the field, looking at exploration and developments and then scouring the financials.

Over the coming weeks and months I toured every facility and project that was in operation and have to say it was very impressive. Caltex’s money would not be wasted and it was quite a coup for them to have achieved this collaboration with IOC.

One of the Indians that I met was a youngish guy called Mukesh Ambani Jr. I thought the junior tag was very American but he was pleasant and engaging. He was more of a listener than most of the Indians that I had met and slowly I came to like and trust this man. At the time, I had no idea who he was, this revelation came much later. I just thought he was one of the management team of whom there seemed so many.

He was interested in my previous projects and I found myself telling him about the North Atlantic and South Africa. He seemed very intrigued by everything I had done. I don't know why but I found myself divulging a lot more than just about the job. Very soon, I had told him about the Accident in the North Atlantic and my discoveries and aspirations with regards to South Africa. I even told him about our plan to try and raise funds to carry on research at the mine just outside Cape Town. He continued to listen attentively to all I had to say.

It is fair to say that he and I became close friends and although I still didn't really know his role within the company, he was always present at every juncture. He was almost like a shadow. In the evenings we would often go out somewhere for a meal and he introduced me to the delights of real Indian curry; all my previous experiences had been from a takeaway in England. He also introduced me to many influential colleagues and friends and I began to feel quite at home in this big city. Perhaps this wasn't too bad after all.

One day, after I had been in India for just over a year, Mukesh said he would like to invite me to go for a long weekend break with him and his sister to Kerala, which he assured me, was a beautiful part of the country.

Although we had been out to dinner on various occasions we had always taken it in turns to pay for our evening. This however, said Mukesh, was a gift as he owned a holiday home.

"Come on, Petrey," he encouraged, "It will be fun and anyway I want to put a proposition to you."

"Ok, Mukesh, I could do with a break from work, it has been pretty intense over the last twelve months. Why not?" I said?

I met up with him and his sister, who had a very European name, Lisa, at the airport. He introduced me to her; she was stunning and I guessed about mid-twenties. She later confided in me that she was 29 and as yet unattached. There was a glint in her eye and a gentle smile as she told me. I wondered if Mukesh was trying a little matchmaking, but if that had been on his mind it was certainly not the main reason for the invitation.

The flight from Delhi to Cochin took a little over three hours and I could see as we came down for the landing how stunning the countryside was. From the air there was a myriad of backwaters, and apparently, historically, the only way to travel around Kerala was by boat. Very soon we had landed and made our way through customs. Many of the officials dotted around the Airport seemed to recognise Mukesh and greeted him cordially.

Then came a number of surprises that I was not expecting. A large limousine was waiting for us, or should I say for Mukesh and his sister. A very smart looking driver chopped my two friends a very sharp salute and I was starting to feel a little confused. Mukesh could see my dilemma and just clapped me on the back and smiled. "Come on, Petrey, smile and relax. All will be made clear very soon."

In the car we made small talk about the lush green grass and trees along the way. I still found it odd to see cows and goats walking along the roads oblivious to the traffic rushing past. And there were Tuk-Tuk's (three-wheeled taxis) of every colour in huge numbers weaving in and out of the traffic and in many cases driving down the wrong side of the road. It was not long before we pulled up outside a large imposing building that resembled an apartment block.

As we entered the foyer there was a flurry of activity as half a dozen people tried to get themselves in the right positions to greet their guests. This was no apartment block but a residence of some importance. I was still feeling overwhelmed and in a state of complete confusion.

A young fellow came and took my case and disappeared into a lift.

"Come on, Petrey let's get ourselves acquainted with the bar," said Mukesh.

This was the most sumptuous bar I had ever seen.

All the fittings for the bar were of light golden oak and the individual chairs also of oak with soft light tan pure leather coverings. The ceiling was festooned with chandeliers which glinted in the bright Indian sunlight showering all areas of the room with hundreds of tiny reflected lights like fairies flitting to and fro.

The back wall of the bar was a complete fitted wine rack and I took several minutes glancing at some of the labels on the bottles. I recognised many of the names but I had rarely been fortunate enough to sample anything like them.

Labels included Mouton Rothschild, Lafite, Latour and many other names that I had heard of and some that I had not.

Behind the bar were two immaculately and uniformly dressed staff, a young man and a young woman. They greeted us all in usual Asian fashion, "Good morning, Miss Lisa, Mr Mukesh, Mr Petrey."

I was still unused to the formal come informal manner of using the Christian name preceded by the title. However I found it quite endearing.

Although there was a huge amount of liquor behind the bar, Thilini served us with a jug of iced fruit drink; she also brought some small snacks not too dissimilar to those offered on airlines. However there were also spicy peanuts and Bombay mix.

I was still somewhat bemused as to what was going on but my confusion was soon to be allayed.

"Petrey, I haven't been entirely truthful with you, and I sincerely apologise for my deception. However, I am very impressed by your work ethic and contribution, and over the last year or so I have learned a great deal about you."

I felt a little uncomfortable and Mukesh could see my discomfort.

"Come on, Petrey, relax this is going to turn out really well once you have forgiven me for my indiscretion. Tell me, have you ever heard of my namesake, Mukesh Ambani?

I thought for a moment or two and then said, "The only Mukesh Ambani I have ever heard of was the guy who became the richest man in the world in 2014, and I believe he had a daughter who was the richest girl in the world at aged just sixteen."

"Perhaps you would like some vodka in your fruit juice," he teased with a broad smile. "It might help you to cope with the next few minutes."

"Come on, Mukesh, stop the secrecy and get on with it," I quipped.

"Well," he mused, "Mukesh Ambani was my Great-Grandfather, and Lisa and I are heirs to his vast fortune."

For a moment I was stunned and flippantly said, "Oh! That explains the chauffeur driven car and this awesome bar. Wow!"

Between them, Lisa and Mukesh filled me in on the details of their upbringing and life as heirs to this fortune. I must have sat spellbound for a couple of hours listening to this intriguing couple who were a delight to be with.

Despite their huge wealth, they were amusing and very down to earth and still enjoyed simple things. Our conversation continued through a light lunch of local seafood and salad which was delicious.

Mukesh said that he enjoyed working in the business without people knowing who he was, not through any deceitful thoughts but so that he could get to know and understand people much better.

The minute anyone knew who he was, a shutter seemed to come down because management and staff alike suddenly became tight lipped and frightened to speak their minds.

"I hope, Petrey, that you are not like the rest of them".

"How often do you bring people on a trip like this?" I asked him.

"Never," he replied.

"In that case I am not like the rest of them." I laughed, feeling much more relaxed now after the initial shock.

This might just be the ultimate in excess. The richest man in the world, Mukesh Ambani and his Wife, Nita, and children lived in the world's largest and most expensive home. Ambani is the head of India's most valuable firm, Reliance Industries, an oil and petrochemicals giant. The home is 4,000,000 square feet and 550 feet high with 27 stories.

Their children were Isha, Anant and Akash.

Great-grandson, born 2048, was also called Mukesh Ambani and both he and Sister Lisa have inherited the family business and wealth.

I guess he had me at a disadvantage because I had divulged most of my life to him including ideas and aspirations that I had. On the other hand, I knew relatively little about him and his family apart from what I had learnt in the last couple of hours.

We spent a great weekend together and I eventually felt totally at ease with them. I have to say that I found Lisa an attractive and congenial hostess. In fact I was beginning to like her a lot. However, I knew that I should not have ideas above my station. Mukesh asked me to keep his identity confidential when I returned to the office, a promise I would keep readily because they had made me feel very special and selfishly I was thinking why would I want to share this special bond with others?

Before the weekend was over Mukesh showed a great interest in my findings in South Africa and was intrigued by the story. He was also fascinated by events in the North Atlantic and the great interest being shown by Washington. When the weekend was over I felt exhilarated and rejuvenated and felt that a new chapter in my life was just beginning.

I found out much later that Mukesh and Lisa felt the same way. Earlier he had told me that he wanted to put a proposition to me but there was no more mention of it and so I left it for the time being, thinking that he would tell me when the time was right, whatever it was!

Monday - and back to work. Mukesh was there, pottering around from department to department showing his interest and expertise in all things. I wondered if any of them had any idea who he was.

That night I called Brendan and told him about my new friends, including the very attractive Lisa and mused over with him if and when I would see her again.

"I think, Petrey, that you are besotted with her," he teased and I admitted that I found her to be a beautiful young woman.

"I have managed to secure some funding for our project in South Africa, but at the moment it is only a small amount and would not get us very far.

"The University is willing to put up about £5,000 and I have found a company who is willing to supply us with a shaft lift capability and all the associated equipment for which they would like to be recognised if there is any good publicity.

"Also Millet's are willing to supply us with all the camping equipment we need plus and endless amount of rope.

"South African Airways will be happy to supply us with flights to and from Johannesburg and will also transport all the equipment we will need to take.

"Although it is some distance away, Kenya Navy had offered to loan us three long wheel base Land Rovers.

"All of them are aware that we may be two years away from this expedition but were still pleased to make the offer unconditionally for up to a period of five years."

When Brendan had started to tell me about his achievements as being only small I was a little disappointed but when he trotted out the full details I was beginning to feel quite elated and excited about it all.

"And I also have some fantastic news about Grace," he gushed. "She has completed all of her 'A' levels a year early, and has won a scholarship to Birdbeck University of London to study Forensic Geology."

I could sense his pride and I was proud also. She was a bright girl and had a great future ahead of her. I asked to speak to her but Brendan told me that she had gone out with some friends to celebrate her academic success.

"You know, Petrey, she gets more like her mother every day and I have to admit it, even brighter and more intense. She is going to break a few hearts on her way through life. Of course I want the very best for her but I am also very protective of her and I am not looking forward to the day she has to go off to University. I know she is sensible but I will worry about her."

"Don't worry too much, Brendan, she will be fine, and she will excel at her studies and make you even more proud. If you ask me you're just going to miss having her around you all the time; perhaps it will do you good. It will give you a chance to get out more and meet new people and make new friends".

"How much longer do you expect to be in India? Or perhaps now that you have a new love in your life you might never leave," chuckled Brendan.

"I am not in love," I answered just a little too quickly.

Brendan promised to keep me abreast of his preparations and sponsors for our future project and with that all discussed we ended our very long call. Thank goodness Caltex paid for all my calls.

I didn't see a lot of Mukesh over the next few weeks as I was busy out in the field studying our latest finds. I had quite a number of samples to sift through which often took me late into the night. Anyway, I arrived home quite late about a month later to find a note on the mat inside my apartment door. I don't know what came over me but as soon as I saw the signature my heart started to speed up and thump excitedly. It was from Lisa, and she wanted to know if I would be available the following Saturday evening to be her escort to a formal function that she had been invited to. She had written down her number and asked me to give her a call as soon as I received her message.

What is up with me, I thought, as I reached for the phone? My hands were trembling with anticipation and I smiled and shook my head. Perhaps Brendan was right and I was feeling a lot more for Lisa than I first thought I did.

"Hi, Petrey, so good of you to get back to me so quickly," she gushed. "I hope it was not too forward of me to approach you like this."

"Not at all, it was a real delight to hear from you." I tried not to let my excitement show too much because I had no idea how she felt about me and I might be letting my strong attraction for her run away with me.

"On Saturday we have all of the top people from Caltex visiting from the USA for a board meeting, but in the evening we are hosting a formal dinner party for them and also the US Ambassador to India and one or two other US dignitaries. Normally Mukesh would take me as his escort but he has been obliged to partner up with one of the American ladies, and anyway he is my brother. It would be nice to have you as my escort so that I can enjoy the evening with someone I know and like."

She seemed a little breathless on the other end of the phone or was it just my imagination. "Anyway, I know you have a dinner suit and I don't have to look around for anyone else." I could hear she was laughing quietly at the other end of the line.

"I will send a car for you at about 7pm and it will bring you here to collect me. Perhaps we could have a drink together on our own before heading off to dinner."

She seemed to have everything organised and I agreed with the arrangements.

The rest of the week seemed to drag by and as I had no real project to work on for the week it made it seem even slower. I was nervous and excited at the thought of spending some time with Lisa but also tried to control the way I felt. After all she was the richest woman in the world, what could she possible see in me? I was probably just one of many escorts she could call on and as it was work related I was a sensible choice for the evening.

The car collected me on time on Saturday evening and we sped off to Lisa's apartment. The apartment was well appointed but not as extravagant as I had expected. She certainly did not flaunt her wealth and I was quite surprised at how practical everything was in there. There was little in the way of fripperies and there were no staff in evidence apart from the driver. I later learnt that she kept house for herself most of the time. Having been brought up with staff everywhere she found it refreshing to be able to spend time on her own without people running to and fro.

We arrived at the Hyatt Hotel and were quickly ushered into the cocktail bar adjacent to the dining room. There were already about twenty or more guests chatting and being introduced and we joined in with the general chit chat.

Mukesh suddenly appeared with a very attractive American lady on his arm and he greeted me warmly and introduced me to his friend. She was the daughter of the US ambassador and was a very warm friendly lady. Mukesh stayed with us for only a few minutes and then drifted off into the crowd.

Before going in for dinner Lisa excused herself and said she needed to go and powder her nose and I also took the opportunity to slip off to the gents' bathroom.

The gents was at the end of an adjoining ante-room and I was only half way across the room when I was suddenly accosted by two large men who hustled me into a nearby doorway so that we were hidden from the rest of the guests.

I was just starting to protest when one of them said, “Be quiet, Mr Jonesy, and listen carefully. We are colleagues of Emio Swarzkof and he needs questions answering.”

“Can’t this be done in a civilised manner?” I retorted angrily.

“It could have been civilised if you had given Emio some answers and we are not willing to wait any longer for you whilst you procrastinate. It is a matter of state and international security that we get some answers from you, and whilst you keep flitting around the globe we have been unable to pin you down.”

“So how did you know where to find me now?” I asked them.

“We are responsible for security of US dignitaries, including the Ambassador, and so we vet the entire guest list to ensure there are no undesirables invited. We got lucky and here you are, not exactly undesirable but on our wanted list of people to talk to.”

At that moment Mukesh suddenly appeared and the two heavies suddenly sprang to attention. “Is everything OK, Petrey?” he asked.

He was frowning deeply and could see that there was unwanted interaction going on between me and the two goons.

“I think these gents have made a mistake and were checking my identity,” I told him. They both seemed unsure of what to do and were well aware of Mukesh’s importance and so made their apologies and departed.

One of them glanced over his shoulder and said, "Nice talking to you, Petrey, perhaps we will get a chance to chat again later."

"Come on, Petrey, what was that all about?" I briefly told him that it was about some work I had done previously and when he had some time to spare I would tell him all about it. I was feeling quite shaken and Mukesh found a waiter and produced a large cognac to calm my nerves. He smiled indulgently.

"Now I thought you were a nice guy, Petrey and here I find you in the shadows consorting with a pair of thugs. I think we have enough of our own thugs in India without you inviting your nice friends," he laughed.

"You go off and enjoy yourself with Lisa and we will have a long conversation about this later, and don't worry I will have them watched for the rest of the evening. You can be assured that they will not bother you again tonight."

"Thanks, Mukesh, I feel relieved about that and I promise I will give you the full details soon."

The rest of the evening was very pleasant and I became acquainted with many top US officials including some jovial old General who had been in India for over thirty years. It seemed he spent his life going to cocktail parties and dinners and had a waistline to prove it.

He kept us entertained about the changes he had seen in India. Then he talked about his Great, Great, Great-Grandfather, who had been around when India won her independence. He showed us a very worn and weathered black and white photograph of a huge pair of tusks that he said adorned the ancestral home back in England. It was a trophy from the old days when elephant hunting was legal and also one of the major sporting activities in India.

We drove back to Lisa's apartment and she invited me in for coffee. By now I was quite tired and still feeling nervous about the unpleasant encounter early in the evening. However, I was the perfect gentleman, and after coffee thanked her for a lovely evening and complimented her on how stunning she looked. She smiled and lifted herself on to her toes and kissed me gently on the side of the face. She escorted me to the door and told her driver to take me back to my apartment, and with a twinkle in her eye she smiled at me and simply said, "Soon."

I could not sleep for the rest of the night, wondering what the Americans meant by state and international security. Also thoughts of Lisa added to my already befuddled brain. The sun was coming up when I must have drifted off into a turbulent sleep and was awoken by the sound of the telephone ringing.

"Hi, Petrey, I hope you were not too busy, James Durbin here."

"Hello, James," I replied. "What are you doing ringing me at this unearthly hour?" I glanced at my watch it was nearly midday, 7am in the UK.

"Well, I am due to leave the Royal Navy at the end of the year and wondered if you had thought any more about our conversation. I have no plans for the future yet and was hoping that you might have something for me."

"Gosh, tempus fugit." I said to him. "To be honest I have been so busy that I really did forget when you were due to retire. It is still a few months away before you finish and I promise I will see what I can do."

We talked for about half an hour and I managed to find out from him that the accident on the Extra had been put down to debris floating just below the surface and all enquiries were fully concluded and no more mention had been made of it at all."

I thought it prudent not to mention my run in with the Americans at this time and thought it would be better to talk to him face to face about it.

I was due to go to England to see my parents in a couple of weeks and agreed to call him when I was home so that we could meet up. I also intended to use that time to visit Brendan and Grace and catch up with the planning of our future trip to South Africa.

It was going to be a very full visit as I only had ten days before I would need to return to India. We had found a new giant oil field in the Arabian Sea, close to the coast at Ahmadabad and I had a plethora of calculations to produce for the forthcoming presentation for the Joint Venture Group.

On the day before my departure to the UK Mukesh and Lisa came to my office. Both looked relaxed and in good spirits.

"Good morning, Petrey, I never did mention any more about the proposition that I had in mind but feel I must discuss it with you before you go."

"Come on, Mukesh, what is on your mind?"

"Well, Lisa and I would like to make you an offer which I hope you will consider whilst you are away. It will give you an opportunity to discuss it with your family and colleagues when you get back home. Perhaps you will return refreshed and in good spirits and ready to accept our offer.

"We don't think it is appropriate to pressurise you into anything right now and so we have had a document prepared with all the details included. Perhaps you would be kind enough to wait until you are on your way home before you open it and in that way we can put no undue pressure on you to make any instant commitments. In the meantime perhaps you would do us the honour once more of having lunch with us as a farewell gesture, and also because Lisa suggested it.

"Petrey, I do believe that Lisa is carrying a torch for you and, if she is, then I would not stand in the way of her happiness.

"Mukesh, you are embarrassing me and I am sure you are making Petrey uncomfortable too."

"Yes I do like him a lot, but I don't need my big brother to act as a negotiator. This is the late 21st century and we no longer need an arrangement for this in India. Anyway I can manage my own love life, thank you."

Poor Lisa, her beautiful olive skin had turned bright red and even I was stumbling to find words to say, so I just grinned stupidly. The awkward moment quickly passed and we went out of the office for lunch.

"Do you like Japanese cuisine, Petrey?" asked Mukesh.

"Yes, I do, and most other international foods as well."

"Good, then we will go for a Japanese lunch; you will love this place, Petrey. I can't take all the credit for this place as it was Lisa who introduced me to its fabulous food."

The car quickly brought us to the restaurant and there was a tastefully lit sign over the door which boasted,

"Izakaya- the first Japanese style fine dining restaurant of its kind in the country. The restaurant offers culinary treasures and fine delicacies from Japan, cooked both in contemporary and traditional style .It brings to India the culture of food from Tokyo, a blend of delicacies to suit every palate.

Once we were inside the restaurant the true quality of the premises was plain to see. It offers a relaxed and serene ambience; the space is clad in shades of exuberant reds, classic black and sparkling gold. A Japanese chochin lamp with Izakaya written in Japanese welcomes the guests at the entrance. Each guest is greeted by the staff with the traditional greeting 'irrashaimase'. The food menu includes an impressive line-up of Sumibiyaki, Yakitori and vast assortment of Sushi, Sashimi, Maki and many more mouth-watering delicacies.

We dined like kings and many years later I still recall that lunch that I shared with Mukesh and Lisa as one of the best dining events of my life. It really was very special. I felt at home with the intelligent wit of Mukesh and the stunning beauty of his younger sister to whom I was becoming more and more attached.

This was a really unique situation and I cannot recall feeling happier in my life. I had no idea that this was just the beginning of a very long, exciting and satisfying friendship.

Lisa sent a car to pick me up at 3.45 in the morning to take me to the airport. The car made a short detour on the way to pick her up from her apartment and she was happy and cheerful despite the early hour. Her hair smelt of Jasmine and I was captivated at her simple beauty that needed no makeup. All too soon the journey to the airport was over and I left Lisa standing watching me go through immigration. She had kissed me gently and wished me a safe journey.

Being so early in the morning, I quickly got settled in for the long flight to London. I decided to forgo breakfast and try and catch up on a little sleep. I briefly heard the Captain say that we would be about twenty minutes late taking off but that we would soon make that time up. By the time we had left the ground I was sound asleep.

I slept soundly for about three hours and was awoken by the hostess offering me a bottle of water and some snacks. She also asked me if I wanted an English newspaper and I took the Daily Telegraph. It made a change to read the English news as I was very much out of touch with things at home. Most of it was just general news and it was good to catch up but there was a small article on page five that caught my eye.

'A number of items have been found in some caves in Iceland, close to Reykjavik, that cannot be identified. They have a metallic base but despite many scientific tests their origins are a mystery. Research continues."

There was little else in the article apart from the name Emio Swarzkof who was the senior science investigator based in Washington.

Oh, good, I thought, perhaps he will be too busy now to bother me.

I suddenly remembered that I had an envelope in my briefcase that Mukesh had handed to me. I thought now would be a good time to take a look at it. It had been handwritten in very neat writing on company headed paper. He must have prepared the letter a couple of weeks earlier because it was dated March 14th 2087.

It began:

Dear Petrey,

Over the past year or so it has been my pleasure to work alongside you and observe the professional way that you carry out your research. I was also touched by your integrity after finding out who I was. Not once did you divulge your knowledge to anyone else in the Company and for that I am most grateful. It has been essential that I am able to further the company business discreetly and securely because of the immense value of our portfolio. I am also aware latterly of Lisa's fondness for you and I am completely at ease with that.

Both she and I have discussed the future as we see it and would like to make you the following proposition.

1. *We would like to offer you a very senior position within our company which would mean you having to resign from Caltex.*
2. *Your salary to be discussed but would be in excess of your current remuneration.*
3. *If you accept this position then immediately on taking up our offer we will give you indefinite paid leave to carry on your research in South Africa.*
4. *We would also like you to accept full finance, (apart from the funding that you have already been offered) for your project which we will fund subject to our own involvement, but not interference.*
5. *Apart from our involvement your team will be entirely at your discretion.*

The ten days that you are away in the UK will give you a little time to discuss these contingencies with your family, friends and colleagues . I sincerely hope that you find the idea to your liking and feel able to accept our offer. If you have any questions whilst you are away then please contact me on my private mobile number. I would also appreciate your total discretion within the company as I would like this operation to be kept private and totally separate from our oil exploration business.

Wishing you a happy time with your family,
Kindest regards, M & L

I was stunned; I had never come across such warmth and generosity. Now my thoughts began to run riot. The possibilities were endless and I could build a team around me to go and follow my dream and find out what had happened to my Uncle and learn the secrets of the African mine. I tried to sleep again but I was far too excited and just lay back in my seat as a million ideas ran amok.

Chapter 13 Planning for the Mine

Mum and Dad met me at Heathrow and we were soon home as they lived about an hour away. It was strange being at home again after such a long time. There were so many memories of being a child and yet I seemed to feel quite a stranger here. I guess I had grown up and moved on in my life. Somehow my parents seemed different and it took me a while to put my finger on it. Going to Israel had changed their lives.

Before that they had been plodding away teaching, month in and month out, year in and year out for decades. Now they had seen something different and had started to realise how I felt about exploring new avenues and new places. I was happy for them. They were now planning to go and live on a Kibbutz next summer for several months and had managed to get released from their school duties for a short time.

They were interested in my career and I told them in great detail about the things I had been doing for the last few years since I had last been at home. However I did not mention my plans to return to Africa. I did tell Dad that I had visited the top of the mine where his brother had been killed, but I said no more. I wasn't sure if he would be pleased I was going back or if I should let things lie.

My two days were quickly over and I had enjoyed my time with them, but I needed to go and see Brendan to discuss future plans, and indeed to tell him of the generous offer that had been made. I said farewell to Mum and Dad and told them it would not be so long next time. Dad took me to the station and I was soon on my way to Aberdeen. Whilst on the train I took the opportunity to call James Durbin to try and work out how I could fit him into my future plans.

He was delighted to hear from me because his time in the Royal Navy was just about concluded and he had been offered a job working in the shipyard at Barrow in Furness. This would have been well paid but he thought that it would not live up to the life he had led whilst in the Service.

It was initially for an annual contract which could be terminated by either party at any time within that period. A more permanent contract would be offered at the end of this period if both parties were happy with the arrangement.

"James, I may very well have something for you but I need a little time to organise it. Please be patient for a little while longer and I am sure you won't be disappointed."

"OK, Petrey, I will leave it in your hands and I trust you."

Brendan was a little late picking me up from the station and apologised about the traffic. He said there had been an anti-Washington rally and the streets had been teeming with people.

"Why an anti-Washington rally, Brendan, has something happened?"

"Apparently Washington have become more and more heavy handed with our own government and their rhetoric has become quite dictatorial. They are demanding access to any data that we may have on UFO's, unusual sightings and anything that might be classed as extra-terrestrial. Our scientists and newspapers have organised this rally to let them know that they are not our masters and that their demands will get a negative response."

"Sounds a bit far-fetched to me, Brendan," I quipped.

"Yes, it might be, but a few scientists have reported that they have been hassled and bullied by American agents and that they have had unsolicited visits to their laboratories and some have even had their families intimidated."

"I'm sure it will soon blow over, Brendan."

"Mmm," he said unconvinced. I did not mention anything to Brendan at the time but I was beginning to feel a little uncomfortable remembering my own unpleasant escapade with the Americans in Delhi.

Grace was away at university and so I did not see her on this visit. Brendan was still elated at her academic results and just as pleased that she had managed to get a place at Birdbeck University. She was now hard at work in her first year and seemed to be enjoying being more independent much to Brendan's chagrin; he was really missing her.

It was early evening and Brendan suggested that we go for a Chinese meal and a nice cool bottle of Pinot Grigio. We ordered a set meal for two and sipped on our wine whilst we waited for the food to arrive at the table.

I was very excited about the news I had for Brendan but let him elucidate on his progress so far. He had received written confirmation from all of our sponsors and the Daily Telegraph had agreed to fund the operation £5,000 per month providing they had a total monopoly on the story. It just needed my signature on the contract that they had drawn up. I agreed to consider it after some more discussion between the two of us.

Just for a few minutes, I had some negative thoughts, and wondered if I had taken on more than I could cope with; but I realised that there was now no going back as there were too many companies and individuals involved. I took a deep breath and produced the letter that Mukesh and Lisa had given me and handed it slowly to Brendan. With a broad boyish grin on my face I said to him, “Read and be amazed.”

He studied the letter for about fifteen minutes and then put it down and spent several minutes in thought before his face cracked into a huge smile and said, “It looks like we are on our way, you genius.”

We spent the next few days planning our operation to South Africa. We both agreed that from now on we needed to keep a journal of everything that we talked about, and of all decisions and actions that we took.

Planning the equipment was probably the easiest part. However we were struggling on the start time and also who to include in our team and how many we should include and what skills we might need.

Initially the plan was to get to the bottom of the mine and try to assess what had gone wrong in both of the tragic accidents. With a record of two very bad disasters, safety had to be of paramount importance in our planning. It was with that in mind that we started to formulate a team. We made two lists, one to include the names of people we thought should be included and the second a list of the skills that we would need.

List One

Mukesh & Lisa Ambani
Brendan Crickley
Petrey Jonesy
James Durbin
Thabo

List Two – Personnel

Mining Engineer
Electrician
Site Foreman
Forensic Expert
Safety Officer
Mechanical Engineer

We were aware that Lisa would be the only lady with us on the operation and so whilst we were looking for our members for List two, we thought it would be a good idea to investigate if there were any wives among the prospective team members who would like to take part in our adventure.

I would have to return to India and so I gave Brendan the huge responsibility for organising everything in my absence. We decided on an approximate time of late 2087 which would give us just over six months from now to be ready to go. It would also be summer time in South Africa which I thought was preferable rather than attempting an operation like this in the winter. I asked him to recruit and interview the members we needed from List Two. I just needed to contact James Durbin and Thabo to ensure that they would be available. Brendan also agreed to deal with permits and whatever visas we might need to carry out an operation of this scale.

We spent the next few days trying to tie up loose ends and I contacted the Caltex team in South Africa to ask them to contact Thabo for me. He had told me that he would always be available if I needed him for anything. After a few hours they called me back to say that nobody knew of Thabo's whereabouts and that he had only been seen once or twice since I had left, and not at all in the last six months.

This was a blow because apart from enjoying his company he was an excellent guide and also ambassador when dealing with local tribes people. I had no other way of trying to contact him and I was hugely disappointed. Who could possibly take his place in my team?

Before my return to India we tentatively set our start date as the 1st November 2087. That is, we intended to be in Johannesburg by that date. Brendan immediately starting putting wheels in motion and communicating our plans to our various sponsors. Kenya Navy said that if we would let them know the time of our arrival in Johannesburg they would make sure that the three Land Rovers with drivers would be available and waiting for us when we touched down.

It would then take us several days to cover the 900 miles from J'burg to Cape Town and although it would have been easier to fly to Cape Town there would have been no sponsorship by South African Airways and we decided that this was a small price to pay.

We would also benefit from enjoying the spectacular scenery and also give the team an opportunity to acclimatise to the African Summer sun. There was also the added advantage of having the Kenya Navy not only sponsoring the Land Rovers but also covering our fuel costs.

The Kenya Navy had decided to air freight the Land Rovers to Johannesburg, worried about the toll that the 2,500 mile journey over very rough terrain might have on the vehicles.

The Kenya Navy also had some other good news for us. They had working with them a young British officer, Lieutenant Chris Phillips, Royal Parachute Regiment. He had been seconded as a liaison officer to the KN which they considered a great honour. Although British, his parents had emigrated to Kenya when he was just a small boy and lived in Nyali, close to Mombassa.

As a young boy he had scrambled around on Mount Kilimanjaro, the highest mountain in Africa at about nineteen and a half thousand feet and later had become a Mountain Leader and part of the mountain rescue team. He had also led a number of teams to the top accompanied by his childhood friend, Jimmy Brind, whose parents had also emigrated to Kenya.

Jimmy lived and worked on the Tsavo Game Park but also helped out at the Mountain Centre at Loitokitok situated on the lower slopes of Kilimanjaro.

Both Chris and Jimmy were fluent in Swahili and a smattering of other African tongues and had asked to be included as part of the Land Rover loan to us. They would drive two of the Land Rovers but would also happy to assist in any way possible. They would hire someone to drive the third Land Rover.

Our team was already coming together and fortunately we were going to have some seasoned operatives working with us. It occurred to me that these two guys, apart from driving the land rovers might also fill the positions of Safety Officer and Site Foreman. Perhaps they didn't need to have those titles but could carry out those jobs between them. It was something we could discuss with them and if necessary meet up in advance to share our plans and requirements.

All too soon I was on my way back to Delhi with very mixed feelings. I was feeling nervous about the future and I wondered if Lisa would still have the same feelings that I had for her. Despite it being only 6.25am my fears were unfounded because a very happy smiling lady was there to greet me on my return and seemed delighted that I was back.

She rushed me back to her apartment where I had a long leisurely shower after my long and sticky flight.

"Are you feeling up to meeting up with Mukesh this evening? He's really wanting to know what you have decided and so am I," she purred.

"Do you want to know now?" I smiled, "Or do you want to wait until we meet up with Mukesh?"

Totally ignoring my question she quizzed, "Well, did you miss me while you were away or were there too many distractions in England?"

"There were many distractions," I teased. "Anyway, I was in Scotland most of the time, and the distractions were my family and friends, nobody else."

"Will I be returning to my apartment tonight or are you holding me hostage," I tried to look serious but had difficulty keeping a straight face.

"That depends on you, doesn't it?" she taunted.

Feeling a little more refreshed we met up with Mukesh at a little after 11 at a small discreet coffee bar that I had not previously visited. The staff greeted Lisa and it was obvious that they knew her as a regular customer but that was all.

After a few minutes of greetings and general chit chat Mukesh said, "Well, Lisa, has he told you anything yet?"

"Not a word," she replied, "He is waiting to tell both of us."

I knew them both well enough to tease them a little. "Well, I have discussed it with Brendan and we agreed it might need more time to contemplate."

For a moment they both looked disappointed and I could not keep up the suspense any longer. “We both thought about it for at least ten seconds, and yes, we would be delighted to accept your generous offer.”

The smiles were back on both of their faces before Mukesh said, “And what about your position with Caltex, will you resign?”

“I have already drafted a letter but I would like you read it before I hand it in, if you don’t mind.” I answered.

“There is another matter I need to discuss with you once you are back in the office.”

“That sounds a bit mysterious,” I said.

“Well, yes, it is a bit.” Mukesh changed the subject quickly and we spent the next hour or so talking about the African project.

I went back to the office with Mukesh, leaving Lisa to go back to her apartment. I promised to go back there later and pick up my case.

Once we were back in my office, Mukesh looked quite serious and said he had received a long email from Emio Swarkskof in Washington.

“Petrey, this guy is not going to let go and insists on meeting you for a face to face discussion about the samples that you provided for him. He was unable to contact you personally because he says you are very evasive. I emailed back to tell him that this was not the case but that you are very busy and never in one place for too long. Do you have any idea what this is all about, Petrey?”

“I am going to have to speak to him I suppose. Washington appear to be getting very heavy handed over a lot of things, there was even an article in the Daily Telegraph about Emio and some samples that had been found in Iceland."

"I think you had better read his email, Petrey, because he briefly mentions Iceland and also some caves in the mountains in the Namib Desert in Namibia."

Sir,

I have been trying to arrange a discussion with one of your colleagues, Petrey Jonesy, who had some samples in his possession that we need to know more about. However, he is being evasive and it has been difficult to meet him face to face.

I cannot disclose too much until I speak to him personally. There have been other similar samples identified in Iceland and now more samples have come to light found many years ago in caves in mountains in the Namib Desert in Namibia. It is vital that we talk to him at his earliest convenience.

Please ask him not to try and evade us any longer or we may find it necessary to have our agents forcibly make him comply. I do not wish to do this but it may become necessary. We believe that this may constitute a threat to International security.

Emio Swarzkof
Senior Science Investigator
For the US Government
Washington

I went back to Lisa's apartment feeling very frustrated at the events of the morning; it seemed to put a dampener on our own exciting project. I discussed it with Lisa and she agreed with me that I should meet with this Emio fellow as soon as possible and clear the air so that I could concentrate on our own planning.

Needless to say, I spent that night in Lisa's apartment.

The following day I contacted Emio and agreed to meet him. He seemed a little more amiable this time and the threatening undertones were gone. He had to come to India to meet with some government officials in about 10 days and we arranged a time and venue for our meeting. I asked if I might bring a colleague and friend with me but he was not too keen on that idea and preferred a one to one meeting for this first occasion.

I joked with him about 'this first occasion' and said I hoped that it would be a once only occasion. He sounded a little more serious when he said that he thought it might need more than one meeting. He said he would explain all when we met and hoped we could overcome our distrust for each other at the same time.

He left me feeling like wayward schoolboy and I felt somewhat tense about the whole affair. However I did intend to read up on the Namib Desert Mountains before our meeting. I had never even heard of them before and knew nothing about them. I didn't want to go into a meeting completely blind.

I tried several search engines and found out quite a lot about the Namib Desert. Just as a note I put together the following:

The highest peak in Namibia is the Konigstein (2,606m) in the Brandberg mountain range.

The Namib Desert is said to be the world's oldest desert.

The sand dunes in the Namib Desert are among the highest sand dunes in the world.

The Arnhem Cave, around 4,500 metres long, is Namibia's longest cave. The National Museum of Namibia maintains a record of all the country's caves.

The Hoba Meteorite, nineteen kilometres from Grootfontein, is the world's largest meteorite. It is estimated that the Hoba Meteorite fell on the earth around eighty thousand years ago.

Fossils of dinosaur footprints, between one hundred and fifty and one hundred and eighty-five million years old, have been designated a national monument of Namibia.

I also found some references to unusual occurrences back at the beginning of the century around 2001. Strange lights had been seen in the sky and on the ground in the area but because of its isolation few people got to hear about it. It had apparently frightened some of the Himba tribe's people, but because of their dislike of most other people it had been some time before this strange phenomena had got back to the civilised world. It was only when the Himba decided to uproot and move further south that questions started to get asked.

It was probably as late as 2004 that a scientific team had entered into the massive Arnhem Cave complex. Although much of the labyrinth of caves had been documented, there were still vast areas of tunnels that no one had ever been in.

During their search of the caves the team had discovered that someone or something had been there and had been there for quite some time but were no longer in evidence.

Whatever it was that had been in there had thoroughly swept the place clean and there was only minimal evidence left for the scientists to work with. They did however have some substances that they could not explain and to this day have never been accounted for.

I read through many more articles about the Namib Desert and it made me think that maybe one day I would go and visit this ancient of all deserts and hills. Nevertheless I was primed with some information for my meeting with Emio in a few days' time.

He stood up to greet me as I walked into his hotel room. I wondered how much money the US Government spent on this type of activity for their agents. To say that it was plush would be an understatement. Lisa's apartment was sumptuous but this was in a class of its own. I could see from the centre of the room as I walked in that even the bedroom had chandeliers.

No wonder governments were failing when they spent this sort of money on business accommodation. Emio Swarzkof was not at all what I had expected. He was much smaller, in fact very much smaller than I had anticipated. I guessed he was about 5 feet 7 inches tall and painfully thin. I wondered if he was ill. However, once he spoke he commanded attention and expected to get it.

"Good morning, Mr Swarzkof," I returned his greeting.

"Emio, please," he cut in. "Do sit down and make yourself comfortable. Can I get you a drink?" he asked.

"Black coffee would be fine, no sugar, thank you," I replied.

He pushed a button on a remote control and within a few seconds an hotel maid came in and took his order.

"Let's get down to business," he said. "Now are you going to tell me about these samples willingly or do we have to do it the hard way?" he smiled charmingly. I wasn't quite sure what he meant by the 'hard way' but I decided it would be prudent to play along.

"I will agree to tell you what I know if in return you tell me what this is all about?"

He studied me seriously for a few minutes before replying to my question.

"Well now, I guess it won't hurt to tell you a little bit about it providing you guarantee that you will not talk to the media about it."

I agreed that if it was in the interests of International security then he could be sure of my integrity.

"The samples that you were trying to analyse, which are the ones we now have in custody are extremely unique and contain certain elements that do not appear to be anything that we have ever come across. They are not the only ones we have, and if you have read any newspapers in the last few months then you will know that this is becoming quite an international incident.

"We have some samples found in Iceland, some in Namibia and the Chinese say that they have some, they will not give us access to them and likewise we will not give them access to ours. It's a stand-off.

"We are of the conclusion that these samples were made or constructed by persons unknown using techniques that are far in advance of anything we have ever seen. What we do know is that whatever the material is made of, it is impervious to anything we have tested on it.

"What we have here, Petrey, is either a group of people who are working independently of governments and their science is extremely advanced or we are looking at visitors from elsewhere."

I wanted to push him on that point. "What do you mean? Elsewhere?" I encouraged him.

"Well for the want of sounding foolish and incredulous, I mean alien, from another planet."

"Is that really likely?" I interjected.

"Well it's all we have to go on at the moment," he replied.

"OK, I have done my bit, now it is your turn, tell all."

Up until this moment I had intended keeping the information a tightly guarded secret but I realised there were far more implications than I had dared to imagine. Of course, I must tell him, I thought to myself but I need to protect James Durbin from any repercussions from this event. I thought the best way would be to tell the truth but say that I had picked up the samples from the cast off metal that James had cut out of the ships side. This way James would be protected and Emio would have his answers.

In the end, that is exactly what I told Emio.

He looked at me thoughtfully and then said, "Petrey, would you write a report for me outlining everything you know about this accident including exactly where you were when this occurred and the time and date plus anything else you can think of that might assist our enquiries."

He said it was of an urgent nature and could it be done expeditiously. I agreed to start immediately and that he would have his report within twenty-four hours.

I now needed to contact James Durbin as quickly as possible and for two reasons. I wanted to keep him abreast of matters with Washington and to let him know that I had been totally discreet and kept his identity out of the frame. Also, I wanted to know how he felt about coming and taking part on our expedition to South Africa.

I told him the truth and that all his expenses would be paid for but there would be little in the way of remuneration whilst we were there.

I tried to keep it as buoyant as possible by asking him if he would be willing on completion to come and work with me in India. He jumped at the opportunity in South Africa but said he would need time to think about the India relocation. I left it like that and told him I would be in touch but to be available from the end of October onwards.

I had given Mukesh and Lisa full details of my meeting with Emio and after I had told them I sighed.

"Perhaps that will be the end of this awful saga now that I have explained it to Emio."

"Let's hope so," said Mukesh, "although somehow I doubt it."

I almost felt at a loose end now, even though there was a lot of work to be done on the oil contract for Ahmadabad. I shouldn't be feeling like this but it was as if the job was getting in the way of my other plans.

Over the next few months there were many emails went backwards and forwards between Brendan and me. He worked tirelessly in putting everything into place and I felt a bit of a fraud whilst he shouldered most of the responsibility. However, on many nights Mukesh, Lisa and I talked until the small hours, fine tuning everything as we went along.

I was keen to meet Lt Chris Phillips and Jimmy Brind and brief them on the operation, and at the end of August Mukesh suggested that I fly to Nairobi and meet up with them and get acquainted. I think my main concern was that they fitted in with the team as all their other credentials were in excellent order.

I arrived in Nairobi on a very warm and sticky afternoon and it was quite a drive from the airport to the Norfolk Hotel in the centre of Nairobi. I had been spoilt in India as all the vehicles were air conditioned but this was an open topped land rover and I could feel myself begin to melt by the time we arrived at the hotel.

I warmed to Chris and Jimmy immediately; they seemed to complement each other. Chris was gregarious, outgoing and likeable and was a natural leader whereas Jimmy was much quieter but with a great inner strength, and a mischievous sense of humour and I knew he would be a great asset to us.

They had grown up together on the outskirts of Mombassa in a very select almost old colonial style area. Both sets of parents had been successful in business and had been able to afford to move there and buy excellent properties and considerable land holdings. They had the privileges of wealth but it had not been detrimental to them in any way. They were intelligent, keen and very down to earth. Both men seemed to know instinctively what I was looking for and I knew that they were the right people for the arduous task ahead of us.

I spent only a few days in Kenya but during that time Chris and Jimmy took me into the Tsavo Game Park on a small private safari all of my own. They used a Kenya Navy Land Rover which gave them free access into the park and as we went in and out the guard saluted us.

It is very much a tourist area and Chris thought that we would have time to visit Kilaguni Safari Lodge where we would get to see many animals feeding at the water hole and enjoy a leisurely lunch.

Kilaguni Safari Lodge is set on a ridge with magnificent views of the rugged Chyulu Hills and the snow-capped peaks of Mount Kilimanjaro.

Kilaguni takes its name from a Kamba word meaning 'young rhino'. The lodge was opened in 1962 and was the 1st safari lodge to be built in a Kenyan National Park.

Situated in the middle of the Tsavo National Park, the lodge was built with volcanic stone and blends into the surrounding savannah landscape. 100m from the main building is a waterhole which is visited daily by herds of elephant, buffalo and plains game.

There are many activities to keep you busy including game drives and bush walks accompanied by the resident naturalist, excursions to Mzima Springs with its crystal clear water, visiting The Rhino Sanctuary and climbing the Chaimu Crater.

There's also the option of just lazing by the pool or treating yourself to a luxurious body treatment - a wonderful way to unwind in the heart of the Kenyan bush.

The view as we drove across Tsavo was truly stunning and we saw many giraffe cantering across the plains with their long ungainly stride, with younger ones trying to keep up.

Occasionally we spotted small groups of Maasai tribesmen in their brightly coloured traditional dress of reds and purples. Less frequently we spotted Maasai women who were dressed even more flamboyantly than their men, all wearing multi coloured dress and adorned with huge amounts of jewellery which included layers and layers of necklaces that looked like gold.

Lunch at the Lodge was a totally new experience. The food was laid out on tables all on different levels with a vast variety of meats and cheeses and bowls of fresh salad still glistening with iced water. On a higher level to the rear of the tables was a plateau of fruits, many of which I could not name and had never seen before.

It was a spread fit for a king. The restaurant was circular allowing all diners the opportunity to view the waterhole whilst they ate; elephant, buffalo and many different species of deer and a plethora of brightly coloured birds enjoyed their lunch alongside us; it was a truly memorable view not to be missed.

I was sorry that I had not brought my camera which was somewhere in my apartment in Delhi gathering dust. What a wasted opportunity.

Chris and Jimmy spent a large proportion of their lives out here in the bush and even to them it seemed to give almost childish pleasure being out in this magnificent wilderness. The beauty of it all was so overwhelming that the rest of the world and its problems just dissipated.

All too soon my very short safari was over and I was on my way back to Nairobi airport for my flight back to Delhi. I shook hands with the two men and they said they were looking forward to their trip south later on in the year. I too was looking forward to working with these two guys.

I felt revitalised again and got stuck back into my work with renewed zeal. I felt now that I needed to get the ground work completed in Ahmadabad and file the report quickly. I also took the opportunity to inform Caltex of my decision to leave them at the end of September giving them sufficient notice to find a replacement for me.

I don't know why, but I chose not to tell them that I was actually defecting as it were, to the other side. It would have been difficult to explain why I needed to do it without compromising my close relationship with Mukesh and Lisa, and the plans we had for other activities not related to the business, and of course my own personal aspirations with regards to Lisa.

Although I had come to know Mukesh and Lisa so very well over the preceding months there were still questions I had about them. Perhaps it was just my curiosity but nevertheless I would find the time to broach the subject. Both of them had their own apartments which were both very well appointed but not what you would expect of the richest people in the world and I wondered why they chose this lifestyle.

I had the chance to find out a lot sooner that I thought. Once my notice had been given Mukesh started to invite me to many other meetings that had nothing to do with the oil industry and I soon realised that he was coaching me into his entire business world. We had not discussed what my new position would be but it was not going to be simply as his geologist.

I had been curious about this huge building that his Great Grandfather had built as his home and yet neither he nor Lisa lived there. In Mukesh's words, it was a 'dinosaur' and very early on he and Lisa had decided that it would not be their home. However it employed a staff of over 600 people and they did not wish to see these people without jobs. Many of them were descendants of the staff who had first started working there when it was built and it was almost a dynasty. Mukesh had worked hard with planners and architects to change the complete concept of the building and in the process not a single member of staff lost their jobs. To say he was a philanthropist was an understatement. There were many attributes of the complex that lent itself to its new designation and so the transformation was relatively simple.

Many parts of the building needed little change as they were already functioning. For instance the private car park was turned into a Prestige and Collectors car sales auditorium. The swimming pool and gymnasium were adapted for club use, and the dining rooms changed into select restaurants and now boasted Chinese, Japanese, Indonesian, French and Italian boutique eateries. Mukesh and Lisa loved antiques and so many of the larger staterooms had been carefully interconnected by large doorways and converted into tastefully decorated museum of Indian artefacts.

"Lisa and I like to live a lot more simply but know we have a responsibility to many people who have been with the family for generations. We both enjoy what we do and the seeds for this transformation were set in motion by our parents. Initially, they had thought that there would be no children and had been trying for many years and then when they finally decided not to try any more, Amma found out she was pregnant with me. She was nearly forty-three when I was born and two years later along came Lisa. At forty-five years of age it took a lot out of her and sadly she was only fifty-four when she passed away."

"And your Father?" I asked.

"He was several years older than Amma although how much we don't know, he keeps his age a complete secret so I guess we won't know until he passes on. He is well and lives quietly in a comfortable house near the village that he was born in. It is just outside Nedumbassery in Kerala. Although he was thrust into the limelight with all his inherited riches, he escaped as often as possible to return south to his native Kerala. You will meet him, Lisa and I get to see him quite often."

Everything now seemed to gather pace at an alarming rate and the emails and telephone calls between Brendan and me increased in length and frequency as our deadline fast approached. Mukesh, Lisa and I were booked on a flight to Heathrow on the 15th October which was less than a week away.

I had hardly noticed the transition but I was no longer working for Caltex and my replacement arrived in Delhi and assumed his duties. He had been well briefed and the hand over was relatively simple.

Brendan was anxious to see me and also to meet our benefactors and so he had driven down to London from Aberdeen to meet us off the plane. It was an unusual meeting, with me greeting Brendan who was so familiar to me, and introducing him to Mukesh and Lisa, who I felt were more like family to me rather than my employers.

The awkwardness of the situation quickly passed and I was pleased to see Mukesh and Brendan in animated conversation as we started the long drive to Scotland. Lisa and I sat in the back of the car and it was not long before Lisa was fast asleep with her head resting on my shoulder.

The new motorway, recently opened from Heathrow Airport cut a swathe in a direct line through England and deep into the Highlands of Scotland. It was a toll road but certainly the quickest route to get us to Aberdeen. The distance was just about 500 miles and with the speed limit of ninety miles an hour, the journey was completed in less than six hours.

The service stations at hourly intervals along the route were very modern and high tech and looked more like space stations than service stations. The standard was extremely high and they were all owned by the road toll company and therefore almost identical. We only made two short stops and I took over the wheel for the last couple of hours.

"Mukesh, I have booked you and Lisa into one of Scotland's finest hotels which I am sure you will find to your liking. I have only asked for Bed and Breakfast because we are going to be very busy for the rest of the days concluding our planning for the trip. If you look in the glove compartment there is a small brochure giving details."

Mukesh retrieved the brochure and read out the details for Lisa to hear.

Overlooking Loch Davan, within the Cairngorms National Park, Glendavan House offers luxurious 5-star bed and breakfast accommodation

Built in 1886 as a shooting lodge, Glendavan House has been updated so that each room combines original Victorian features, with state-of-the-art modern facilities.

Each room has bespoke or antique furniture, a digital TV, DVD and CD players, and free Wi-Fi and many rooms have views of the park.

A full Scottish breakfast made using fresh local produce is available and a continental breakfast can be served in the room.

Aberdeen Airport and city centre are an hour's drive away. Balmoral Castle and Royal Lochnagar Distillery are both 12 miles away.

"It is about half an hour's drive in the car from the hotel to my home where we will be spending most of our time."

"It will be nice to stay there and see a little bit of Scottish culture whilst we are here," said Lisa.

We all went back to Brendan's house where a surprise dinner had been prepared for us by none other than my Goddaughter Grace. She was so grown up and sophisticated now and well into her second year at University. It was half term, and she had wanted to come home to see her Dad, and I was really pleased that she had wanted to see me as well. I think she wanted to try her knowledge of geology on me, and ask me for an opinion of how I thought she was progressing. I don't know about her geology but her cooking was excellent and she and Lisa became instant friends and I was pleased that I had Grace's approval.

That evening I called James and asked him if he was going to be able to come and join us. It would give him a chance to meet Brendan, Mukesh and Lisa.

Of course, I wanted everybody to click as it would make a much better experience for all of us. I also contacted South Africa again and my old Caltex colleagues. They had heard that I had left the company and wished me well for the future. They said that they had tried again and again to find out Thabo's whereabouts but even his wives didn't seem to know where he was.

Although I was no longer working with them, John and Madoda said they were looking forward to meeting with me again and suggested that maybe whilst in South Africa we could perhaps enjoy an evening together. I agreed that it would be nice but made no firm commitment.

I was somewhat concerned about Thabo and hoped that he was OK. It certainly seemed strange that nobody seemed to know of his whereabouts. I would definitely make enquiries whilst I was in Cape Town. I was also wondering how we would manage to communicate with the Nama tribes' people, something that Thabo was so adept at, apart from his other obvious skills. He was also great company and I was saddened that we would not have him with us.

James arrived early the following morning and after introductions all round we quickly got on with the planning.

Over the next couple of days we started to tick things of our huge list. Fortunately, Brendan had a very large double garage which we were using as our store. It resembled an enormous hardware store and included rope, knives, leather work gloves, safety hats, torches, head-lamps, work boots, emergency food packs, sleeping bags, waterproof bags, small gas stoves, matches in waterproof bags, a box of cheap gas lighters. The list was seemingly endless and Brendan checked it all thoroughly before we carefully packed everything in wooden crates.

The cage and wire pulley system that would be awaiting us at Johannesburg was completely self-contained and could be hitched to the back of one of the Land Rovers and towed.

The plan was to unload the crates in Johannesburg and unpack them at the airport. South African Airways had agreed to give us part of an old hangar to use to unpack crates and use as storage.

That evening we all went over our personnel list to make sure that we had covered all angles.

We had been very fortunate with our search for a Mining Engineer and Forensic Expert in finding Mr and Mrs Swart (Pieter and Rosa). Pieter was not only a mining engineer but had been involved with examining the mine after the tragic accident in which Uncle Carl had been killed. He was now retired but volunteered his services. His wife, Rosa, was twenty years his junior and they had met at a government department Christmas party many years ago. She had worked for the forensic department but after cut backs in personnel worked now only on a self-employed basis. She openly agreed that she earned more money this way and also had more free time. I was more than delighted that we would have at least one more woman in the team.

I decided that before we started the project we would sit down for a day with the Swart's and get their feedback on the mining accident. It might give us some insight into what we might expect.

Chris called us with news that he could provide a Mechanical Electrical Engineer if we still needed one. The Kenya Navy had a young and gifted black African who took care of all the vehicles and was responsible for the air conditioning supplies at the Navy headquarters in Nairobi. He also helped out where necessary on the Fast Patrol Boats where the output was Direct Current (DC). He currently had a young apprentice whom he was training to do everything that he did. I graciously accepted the offer.

Chris told me that all his plans were up to speed and he would be leaving for Johannesburg in a few days and looked forward to seeing us there. Apart from a few minor adjustments at the last minute, we were just about ready to go.

The night before our departure we went to one of Aberdeen's finest restaurants, knowing that it might be quite some time before we enjoyed any good cuisine again. Brendan chose La Lombarda Restaurant hoping that it would suit all our tastes. It was the ultimate fine dining experience on which we all agreed and we ended the evening with a toast to our success.

The oldest Italian restaurant in Aberdeen, La Lombarda is a family-run business established in 1922. With ample white, red and green in the colour scheme and terracotta accessories, there's something intrinsically Italian about the décor.

Known for its warm ambience, La Lombarda is usually the favourite of families looking to spend quality time with each other. Italian opera music plays softly, setting the mood for laughter and exchange of stories. Aberdeen's close proximity to the North Sea is evident in the extensive menu that has a host of delicacies from the bottom of the ocean.

Seafood lovers shouldn't miss sampling the seafood salad that has everything from mussels and cockles to squid and tuna.

Grace was the only one of our party that night who would not be coming with us but she knew that she had to return to university in London to complete her studies. Nevertheless, she was a little sad at the thought that we were going without her and also that we were taking her Dad away from the UK.

Early the following morning Brendan and I took Grace to the station to get her train to London. She was a little teary on leaving and clung on to Brendan.

"Dad please be careful and come home safely," she said trying to stop herself from crying.

"I will," he assured her.

I kissed Grace gently and promised her I would look after him.

"Oh by the way," she said, "I do like Lisa and I think you make a lovely couple."

I hugged her. "Thank you, Grace, I am really happy that you like her, it means a lot to me."

We waved to her until the train was out of sight and drove back thoughtfully to Brendan's.

Whilst we were at the train station Lisa, Mukesh and James had waited for the truck driver to arrive and load our crates for the journey to Heathrow.

Chapter 14 Return to the Mine

By the time we arrived back at Brendan's, the truck was on its way south. We only had to pack our few remaining personal items and wait for the taxi to take us to Aberdeen Airport for our own trip to Heathrow Airport. The taxi was early and arrived at 10.15 and in plenty of time for us to get to the airport for our flight at 11.45.

The flight from Scotland was only about one and a half hours and would get us there with several hours to spare before our flight to Johannesburg. We just hoped there was no delay on the road and that our crates would arrive in time. We were beginning to wonder if we should have sent them the previous day. As it happened there was little to worry about and we later found out that the crates had been delivered to the loading bay by 4.30 in the afternoon ready for despatch on our 5.35 flight.

We had several hours to kill and wandered around the Duty Free shops. There was nothing that I wanted and so Lisa, James and I went off to Costa Coffee whilst Mukesh and Brendan went off to look around jewellery shops. They joined us for coffee about half an hour later.

Mukesh had found a deal that he could not resist. He had located some 22 karat gold medallions of the Hindu God of Good

Luck, Sri Ganesha. With each medallion was a tiny written scroll made of papyrus.

> ***Ganesha – Elephant-Headed God***
>
> ***Ganesh is the Ever-Blissful, elephant-headed deva (god) who is lovingly worshipped and revered by millions of people worldwide.***
>
> ***Although Ganesh is known through the Hindu religion, Shri Ganesh transcends religion and is loved by many non-Hindus. Ganapati is worshipped by both Vaishnavas (devotees of Vishnu) and Saivites (devotees of Shiva). This is the Transcendent, All-Embracing, Auspicious Lord of the Ganas, Sri Ganesh.***
>
> ***Enjoy and much Peace to you!***

He must have spent a fortune because he had bought one of these unique and delightful talismans for each and every one of the team. It truly was a heartfelt gesture and we all appreciated it. He gave us ours immediately and put the others in his carry-on bag to give to the rest of the team later on.

We had more coffee and talked excitedly about the adventure ahead of us. The time passed very quickly and in no time at all we were boarding our flight to Johannesburg. The journey to Johannesburg was about eleven hours but they were in time zone known as SAST (South Africa Standard Time), this is two hours ahead of GMT and so we would arrive at our destination at 7.45 on the morning of Saturday 1st November 2087.

The were some heavy white clouds as we started to descend into Johannesburg but once we were below them the scenery was breath-taking as we came into land on a bright and warm summer's morning.

It took us little time to clear immigration and customs and we were soon out of the airport and looking to see if our Land Rovers had arrived. About fifty yards from the airport entrance we could see three khaki-coloured Land Rovers and wondered if these could be our vehicles. They were, as we saw Chris and Jimmy striding quickly towards us.

"Good morning Chris, Jimmy," I greeted them and we all shook hands as I introduced them to the rest of the team, and within minutes everyone was chatting animatedly.

"You have brought great weather with you."

"I don't know about that," quipped Jimmy. "It poured with rain all day yesterday whilst we were waiting for the flight down here and only cleared up a couple of hours ago."

"Come on, let me introduce you to our engineer, Abasi, and our third driver," said Chris.

We strode over to where there were two black Africans, one was standing upright by the front of one of the Land Rovers but the other had his head buried inside the hood of the car tinkering with the engine. As we approached he came out from under the hood and for a few seconds I stood there dumbfounded. His face cracked into the most enormous grin as he came to greet me; it was Thabo and, oh boy, was I pleased to see him. Judging by the way that he hugged me I think he was pleased to see me too.

"Hello, Jona-Baas," he chuckled, "fancy seeing you here."

"You rascal," I chided him, "where have you been?"

"I will tell you the story later," he said, "after we have sorted out the crates. Chris has briefed me on the plan so far but now you are here I can take each day as it comes. Jona-Baas, it really is good to see you, I had thought for a while that you would not return but I should not have doubted you."

More introductions all round and Thabo was all smiles and nodded approvingly when I introduced him to Lisa. I looked at him quizzically and said, "What?"

His smile broadened into another of his huge grins as he touched his nose and said, "I can see these things," he laughed, "Remember I have many wives."

"How many now?" I teased.

"Only six," he said, "I cannot keep on getting married, I am getting older, no energy left. Anyway I have enough land and cows now, I don't need any more."

We had to kill a couple of hours to wait for the crates to be unloaded and moved into the corner of an old hangar at the perimeter of the airfield. A South Africa Airways official was waiting for us and Brendan signed all the paperwork. On completion he handed us a copy of the agreement and wished us good luck and said that the agreement was open ended and there was no time restraint on our use of the hangar. Brendan thanked him and he was on his way.

Chris, Jimmy and Thabo brought the Land Rovers into the hangar whilst the rest of us wrenched the crates open. Lisa armed herself with a pad of paper and a pen so that she could list each item loaded into the rovers.

The self-contained unit with the hoist and associated equipment also arrived and this was hitched up to one of the Land Rovers, but not before it had been thoroughly inspected by Abasi. The rest of the day was spent in making three separate piles prior to loading.

The plan was that James and I would travel with Thabo, Mukesh with Chris, Brendan would go with Lisa and Jimmy. We would arrange the space in the back of the Land Rovers to make room for sitting space

James liked the idea of travelling in the back saying that he could have a sleep on route. Knowing African roads, I doubted he would be doing much sleeping.

It took us most of the day to pack all the things neatly into the back of the Land Rovers. They were long wheel base and it was surprising how much we could pack in. Everyone worked hard and we were all exhausted by late afternoon apart from Thabo who seemed to always have boundless energy. There were many times when this seemingly inexhaustible man proved to be one of our greatest assets.

Jimmy slipped away from the group about an hour before we finished packing to see if he could find us all accommodation for the night. We did not need anything five-star, but somewhere clean and comfortable, as it was only going to be a one night's stay, leaving at the crack of dawn in the morning. He was back just as we were packing the empty crates away in the corner of our hangar space.

He had found us a place to sleep about twenty minutes' drive from the airport and the landlady had agreed to get up very early in the morning to cook us breakfast.

Gracious, spacious and quietly gorgeous is the simplest way to describe this magnificent guesthouse in the exclusive suburb of Sandhurst in Sandton, Johannesburg. Elizabeth Manor offers Bed and Breakfast or Self Catering accommodation.

Thabo was unsure about staying in a hotel as he had never done so before and said he would be more comfortable in his Land Rover. He agreed to have dinner and breakfast with us but insisted that for the security of vehicles and their contents it would be better all-round if he remained with the vehicles overnight. I did not want him feeling uncomfortable and agreed that he could do as he wished. As it turned out it was the right thing to do because as we slept that night several cars in the immediate area were broken into and the contents pilfered.

We were all quite tired by the time we had eaten and apart from Mukesh, Brendan, Abasi and me everyone retired immediately after dinner.

Abasi went off with Thabo to the vehicles saying he would be back in a while to sleep. It was odd seeing Thabo sitting at a dinner table but despite his protests that he was not versed in Western culture, his table manners were perfect and I felt sure that he must have done this before.

After a full cooked breakfast we set off on our way. I guess this really was the beginning of our great adventure. Never in our wildest dreams did we imagine where it was going to lead us. It was the start of an incredible journey and even now many years on I have to pinch myself to remind me of how real it all was.

The route down to Cape Town was simple and straight forward and most of the roads were in excellent condition. Nonetheless, often parts of the road became broken due to torrential rain and flash floods. Also occasionally the flooded roads had to be circumnavigated because the water was too deep.

The plan for the route was to try and complete the journey to Fish Hoek in three days. Pieter and Rosa would be there on the third day to join us. Then finally our team would be complete. The following two nights we managed to find some suitable stopping points and Thabo quickly set up an instant working camp. He seemed totally in his element organising and planning a campsite. He was also at ease cooking for nine as he was for just two.

I was a little worried that once we had set up camp near to the entrance to the mine shaft that we might not have enough manpower. We would have all the technical know-how but we might need more people.

As we sat relaxing after our first night on the road, Thabo came over and sat next to me on a sawn off tree stump.

"What are you worried about Jona?" he asked.

I told him that if all went well it would be fine but what would I do if I suddenly needed a working party.

"Nothing to worry about," he smiled. "I can bring you as many people as you need from the Nama village nearby, they trust me and I have told them about you and I only have to ask and they will give us anything we need."

"Thabo, you are such a comfort and I know that if you had not come on this venture we would have struggled to achieve our goals."

"You knew I would come," he grinned.

"Well I had hoped so," I answered him. "But you did give me a scare when I couldn't find you."

"I had to leave the area for a while although things are better now. Two of my Wives decided to have a fight and it became very aggressive and bloody. Then their brothers joined in and all of a sudden I had a feud on my hands. I brought in many of my friends from a nearby village and after a short but bloody battle we quelled the situation but not before three of the brothers ended up with broken legs.

"They put out a blood contract on my head and I had to get away before they finished me off. I travelled up to Kenya and Abasi befriended me, and got me accepted as a driver with the Kenya Navy. I have since paid much money and the contract has been removed and I am now accepted back in my home village. Because the pay was good, I decided to stay. I could not believe my luck when I heard that you were coming back to the mine and that the Kenya Navy had offered to help. I believe for me it was meant to be.

"All of my wives are much better off because they look after the cows and the chickens and the land and I bring in lots of money to help them." He chuckled loudly, "And they all seem much more grateful when I stay with them for a night here and a night there."

It was late afternoon on the 4th November 2087 when we finally rolled into Fish Hoek. Mukesh had a long chat with Thabo about the journey ahead into the hills and then he suggested to me that it might be a good idea to rest up here for a couple of days before setting off on our journey into the lush hills that adorned the distant horizon.

The countryside was stunning and the warm sun just dropping over the horizon looked like a huge orange disk in the sky. All across the tops of the trees was a red glow and it almost seemed as if the nearby dense forest was on fire. I loved the sunsets that settled down so close to us here in the bush.

As the sun disappeared there was a cacophony of sound as all of the animals, birds and bats seemed to recognise the nightfall and aired their lungs for one last time before the long night ahead.

Pieter and Rosa had arrived earlier in the day and had gone off for a short evening walk when we arrived. They soon returned and introductions were made all round. They were a very relaxed couple and fitted into the team very easily. It took a little time to get used to their very strong ‘Yarpie’ accent.

John and Madoda, my two ex-colleagues from Caltex were also there to greet us. Because we decided to stay for a couple of days, Madoda quickly rigged up an electric supply for our campsite. We intended making the most of it because from now on it would be torches and kerosene lamps.

The two days that we spent at base camp were relaxing and fun and we made the most of it, knowing that there was a lot of work ahead of us. Lisa and I managed to go for a walk in the moonlit evening although Thabo had warned us to stay close to the trees and not venture out onto the open plain. As the moon comes up the smaller of the big cats make the most of the shadows to hunt large game which they would not be able to catch during daylight hours.

During our walk Lisa stopped and sat down on the bank of a small stream. ”Come and sit with me, Petrey, we don’t get much of a chance to talk these days with so much going on and I know we are going to be very busy for the next couple of weeks or more.

“Petrey, thank you for being part of my life, I hadn’t realised how lonely I was before I met you. I have all the money in the world and yet it didn’t make me happy. You have brought fun, excitement, travel and incredible goals into my life and most of all, romance.”

I didn’t know what to say, I knew I was falling deeply in love with her but I didn’t dare to hope that it was reciprocal.

“Lisa,” I said quietly, “I love you too. Of course I know about your wealth but sometimes I wish it was not there because I don’t want you or your family thinking that I am only interested in your money.”

“I know you’re not,” said Lisa with tears in her eyes. “Do you really love me?”

“Of course I do,” I replied hugging her tightly to me and kissing her gently.

“When this project is over can we go away on our own for a few days and discuss our future,” she said with a tremble in her voice.

“I think that sounds like a good idea,” I said with a broad smile on my face.

“Before we go back and join the others I have to tell you that Mukesh likes you a lot and is very happy for me to be with you, so you will not get any objections from him, and, believe me, he is very protective of me.”

I didn’t need to reply; I just smiled again and squeezed her hand.

We could smell the food cooking from a long way outside the camp and I knew that Thabo was hard at work preparing dinner for us all. Several of the team had offered to help him but in the end only Rosa managed to persuade him to accept any assistance. Rosa could speak Xhosa including some of the more difficult clicking sounds that few Westerners managed to master. Thabo loves to talk and so was completely in his element chatting with Rosa. Pieter could speak the language a little but not fluently like his wife.

Just a couple of hundred yards from the camp we found a deep stream with fresh cool running water. On a large bend it had formed into a small lake and was safe for swimming and we all took advantage of this safe haven to cool off at the end of the day. We had been lucky that there had been several afternoon thunderstorms that clear quickly, leaving a warm, earthy, uniquely African smell in the air.

Our two days of relaxation were soon over and we quickly reloaded the vehicles. Each time we became better at loading and unloading as we became more familiar with all of the equipment and what was needed and when.

John and Madoda wished us good fortune and waved us off as we slowly pulled away from base camp. We were on our way and I felt suddenly quite nervous about the days ahead. The first day we managed to get across the plain and could clearly see the hills in the distance. The afternoon thunderstorms formed shallow lakes in places and we frequently had to skirt around them so as not to get bogged down and this slowed our progress a little.

We were approaching a place where we had stopped previously, and Thabo with pinpoint accuracy led us into a small clearing. Unfortunately, we were not the only ones planning on settling here for the evening. Without any warning there was a lot of commotion and noise, and then a fully grown rhinoceros with her baby close on her heels came charging at the leading vehicle being driven by Thabo. He swerved to try and avoid her but she skewered the front of his vehicle like a knife going into butter. She turned quickly and ran off with her baby but not before she had left the radiator spurting hot water everywhere.

We had made a grand entrance into our first night's camp. Thabo was angry with himself for not noticing the signs of her being there and muttered angrily at himself. He soon calmed down and Abasi quickly got out his toolbox and set to work on the damaged radiator.

By the time Thabo and Rosa had a meal prepared Abasi was washing his oily hands having repaired the damage. It seemed to me that the skilled team I had around me were extremely efficient and this augured well for our future.

We didn't travel as far on the first day as we had when Thabo and I had done it alone but that was due to the tropical rain that had fallen making the going a bit harder. There were also three vehicles with one towing the hoist engine and that also slowed us up.

As we settled down for the night memories came back to me of how loud the night was. The sounds of all the animals seemed to increase after dark and they all seemed like they were just a few feet away. Thabo was relaxed and animatedly told us what every sound was and how far away he thought they were. We all eventually dropped off to sleep and there were no more incidents that night.

The following morning we passed the rock where I had previously encountered the snake but he was nowhere to be seen. Perhaps it was even too hot for him or maybe a large bird had carried him off and devoured him for lunch.

Now the going started to get more onerous as we began our slow climb up into the hills. Several times we had to stop and unhitch the hoist and manhandle it before re-attaching it again and moving on.

We reached the top of the mine mid-morning on third day and now the work could really begin. Thabo went to scout around the area to find a suitable place for a long term camp. He was gone for most of the rest of the day returning just before dark.

Everyone gathered round as Thabo described the area he had found which was also close to one of the larger vent holes that the Himba had talked about earlier. It was about two miles from our current position but as it was now getting dark a quick camp was erected for the night.

It was an unusual night and there were many loud animal noises, moaning noises and the crashing noises of trees falling, or so it seemed. After the camp was completed Thabo disappeared into the jungle to see his tribal friends and to let them know that we would be here for a long time. He returned about midnight and we told him of the strange noises. He laughed and just said, "Himba tactics."

When pushed for more information he said that the Himba continued to be frightened of westerners and tried to make life as uncomfortable as possible for any intruders with the hope that they would be frightened away.

We slept much better knowing that it was just a ploy. However, in the morning we realised that they would not give up easily. Whilst we had slept they had dug many small holes around the perimeter of the camp and filled them full of a sweet liquid which encouraged thousands of creepy crawlies, mostly of the stinging type.

We were a little amused at the tactics because our camp was only temporary and we intended to move on after breakfast, however it did make us aware that in our new camp we would have to be more vigilant. We either had to deter them or try and win them over to our side.

Mukesh spoke at length with Thabo and I could hear Thabo laughing loudly at something Mukesh had said. Still laughing Thabo disappeared in the direction of the village of his friends.

"What was that all about?" I challenged Mukesh who was still smiling.

"I am hoping we can find a way to get closer to Thabo's friends who will ultimately get us closer to the Himba," he replied.

"So how do you think that can be achieved," I asked him.

"I asked Thabo if there was any way that we could convince them that I was a Herero. With my dark skin I might get away with it," said Mukesh.

"Why would being a Herero cut any ice with the Himba," I asked.

"After you had told me about the Himba tribe I did quite a lot of research and read up on their history," he replied.

"Well it is quite simple really. Between 1904 and 1907 the Germans carried out genocide on the Herero killing about 100,000 of them. The Herero live in the highland areas of Namibia and they live in quiet harmony with the Himba. If the Himba believe that I, as a Herero would befriend your team they are more likely to leave us alone and may even assist us. The Himba are also believed to have descended from the Herero. Their fear is founded on distrust of any western man, believing that they are just waiting for an opportunity to wipe them out," said Mukesh.

Both Rosa and Lisa thought it was worth trying but as the rest of us were men we were a little sceptical.

"Rosa and Lisa are right." countered Chris, "What do we have to lose?"

"Our heads maybe," joked James.

It was time to make Mukesh look a little more acceptable if we were to pull off this ruse. Herero people like others in southern Africa wore clothing made of leather. Men wore different kinds of leather aprons, and male Herero's wore special pieces of animal fur and other ornaments.

Thabo worked hard on the village elders to get them to convince the Himba that we would not harm them and that one in our midst was a Herero. He returned from the village with leather and furs so that Mukesh would look authentic. The senior elder from the village suggested that Mukesh not allow the Himba hear him talk because it would give the game away.

For their part the Nama villagers let it be known that a mute Herero was assisting the foreigners at the mine and that they meant no harm to anyone.

That day we moved into the area that Thabo had found and it was a natural campsite. Rocks bounded three sides of the area with a semi-circle of trees protecting the fourth side. It could easily be protected from intruders of both animal and human types. It was encouraging that from this day on the Himba did not try and usurp us from the camp. The other advantage of this site was that less than 100 yards away was a substantial vent hole leading into the mine.

We knew that we would not be able to open up the top of the mine because the explosives had done their job and the main entrance was completely sealed.

All the equipment would need to be moved through the vent hole and brought to the main shaft. Chris and Jimmy said they would like the opportunity to explore the upper end of the mine thoroughly and prepare a detailed map of the whole area and along with Pieter and Rosa we all agreed that this would be a good plan. Brendan and I asked that they also prepare emergency contingency plans in the event of a rock fall, cave in or any other emergency.

Chris believed that he needed about four days to complete the initial survey. We were all painfully aware that many lives had previously been lost in this mine and did not want any further repetition. I voiced this point quite vociferously knowing that Uncle Carl's life had been taken by this mine.

Abasi unpacked the electric hoist, cage, wire coils and all other associated equipment and laid it all out and inspected every inch of the wires and checked and re-greased all of the moving parts of the cage and pulleys. He ran the electric motor and monitored the temperature for several hours without a load and then again bringing the weight up to the highest possible Safe Working Load.

The team decision on this was that we would never exceed more than half the Safe Working Load at any time, always erring on the side of caution. In real terms that meant that it would never carry more than three personnel or the equivalent weight. (600 pounds maximum, SWL 1,275 pounds.) Safety was our benchmark.

The distance from the vent entrance to the shaft was over seventy-five feet and much of it was just soft soil and rocks some weighing up to 200 pounds. James set about shoring the tunnel so that there was no danger of a cave in. This was made even more difficult because of the recent rainfall that had made the soil even softer than usual and in several places there were small pools of water.

The job was considerably bigger than anticipated and Thabo had to drive back to Fish Hoek to pick up a petrol driven saw. I had managed to contact John and he was kind enough to have one brought to their local office. Thabo and James then selected a number of trees and cut them into suitable sizes for shoring.

Thabo would frequently disappear into the jungle to go and visit the village. Each time he returned he brought something back. The villagers wanted to help and provided us with fresh meat on a regular basis. The village women also collected a luscious variety of local fruits and we were totally overwhelmed by their generosity.

Quite often now one or two of the villagers came closer and closer to us at our campsite and they would play a little game of letting us see them and then dart under cover. Thabo tried to encourage them to come in and make friends but he had his work cut out to entirely convince them that they had nothing to fear.

Mukesh played his part well and paraded around the camp in his leather and furs. It was a source of mirth to us all to see him dressed like that but it started to pay off. It became a bit of a stand-off game with Thabo's villager friends on one side and the Himba on the other side taking it in turns to be seen.

We were now nearly ready to start our initial descent into the mine. Thabo was invited to visit the Himba. He was accompanied by the elders of the village and they honoured him with a banquet. The Himba believed that he must be an important man if he could be friends with the white men, the local village elders and also the Herero that was with us.

This was the breakthrough that we needed because from this point they gave Thabo all the help that was needed. We learnt much about the mine and its history. They could also advise us about flooding and ventilation and they also agreed to open up all the ventilation shafts to increase the air flow throughout the mine.

Moving the hoist engine and all of the heavy cables was going to create a logistical problem because of its sheer weight and the distance it needed to be moved along the vent shaft. Thabo asked the villagers if they would help but they were still not sufficiently comfortable with being too close to us. Fortunately they were happy to work alongside Thabo and Abasi.

The rest of our team moved away from the vent and with Abasi giving Thabo technical advice, Thabo issued instructions to the young men of the village and everything was moved along the vent into place at the head of the mine shaft. It took them just a little over an hour and the cumbersome engine was in place.

We had been in Africa for two weeks now and at last, on the 14th November 2087, all of our plans were complete, all the equipment was in place, Chris and Jimmy's detailed survey finished and it was time to start our descent into the dark depths of this intriguing derelict mine.

Lisa had taken on the role of journalist and was keeping a detailed diary of events. Her task became a little more difficult because there were several events happening at the same time and at different venues.

Whenever possible the team would try and get together and discuss everything that had occurred so that Lisa could be given as much detail as possible. It was often too dark for her to write everything down and she had to rely on our memories to relate details later.

Rosa and Pieter Swart were responsible for photographing every aspect of the operation, particularly the technical detail. Lisa also took general photographs to accompany the diary.

Pieter insisted that all decisions regarding mine safety were his responsibility; negotiating bends in the shaft, rock falls and water obstacles. He was going to be kept very busy.

Thabo and James were to remain on the surface. In the event of a problem Thabo would be able get local help. James was going to continue to cut wood for shores should they be needed further down in the mine.

The plan was to get to about 4,000 feet which is nearly half way down and also the lowest point which the Himba had reached. There we planned to store emergency stores and equipment and it would also give the team a chance to acclimatise to this strange environment. Only Pieter and Rosa had ever been down to a depth of 8,000 feet before.

The rest of the team approached this new challenge in different ways. Lisa was nervous and admitted to being scared. Chris and Jimmy saw it as a challenge that would add another level to their vast mountain experience and they couldn't wait to go down. Brendan had become very quiet and it was difficult to read his feelings. Mukesh approached it as a business project and his brain was working overtime on how the project could be improved on next time. Abasi showed no emotion at all and concentrated on the smooth running of all of his precious equipment. But then Abasi wasn't descending into the mine.

As for me, it had taken a long time to reach this juncture and a lot of time and effort gone into its planning and execution. I was frightened, excited, elated and full of expectation and saw it as the biggest challenge of my life. I knew that none of us would be the same afterwards. It was certainly going to be a life changing event.

Chris and Pieter would go first carrying candles, kerosene, matches torches, spare batteries, blankets, extra clothing and baskets of food and drink.

Abasi had given the hoist a dual control system that it could be operated externally and also in the cage. The cable also had an inner core which contained a telephone cable that would allow communication from the cage to the top of the mine at all times.

Chapter 15 The Terror Below

We almost held our breath as Pieter and Chris disappeared into the gloomy darkness of the mine. A cold chill ran up my spine and I looked around at my brave stalwarts who were putting their lives on the line to satisfy my stubborn and probably reckless dreams. At that moment a feeling of abject terror gripped me and I felt utterly helpless as if I had started something dreadful that I was unable to stop.

The feeling ended abruptly as the cable on the hoist suddenly stopped. Chris and Pieter had reached their destination and were clambering out of the cage into the side vault at 4,000 feet. It had taken them about forty minutes to complete their journey.

Abasi had connected the phone line to a speaker and we suddenly heard the eerie sound of Chris's voice confirming that they had reached their destination. It only took them a few minutes to unload before we heard Pieter's voice over the loudspeaker loud and clear.

"Cage is returning to the surface."

The cables began to move and we waited the forty minutes it would take to return. Then without warning we saw the top of the cage appear out of the gloom.

Mukesh, Lisa and I went next and we descended in total darkness to join our colleagues below. It was an eerie feeling and all we could hear was the whirring sound of the motor as we continued down.

My heart was palpitating and I kept holding my breath as we descended, then suddenly remembering to breathe. In the still silence it sounded as if I was hyperventilating. None of us said a word until the cage stopped and Pieter unclipped the cage door. We stepped out into what felt like a huge dark chilling crypt.

Next down were Jimmy and Rosa leaving Abasi to man the controls. Abasi had chuckled and said that the mine was far too black for him to enter.

“Where’s Brendan,” I quizzed Jimmy as he stepped into the brightly lit cavern.

“At the last minute he said he needed to talk to Thabo urgently and would come down later.” Jimmy replied.

“How strange,” I muttered mostly to myself.

I grabbed the phone and said to Abasi, “Is Brendan there?”

“He is outside talking to James and Thabo, I’ll go and get him for you.”

Brendan quickly came on the phone.

“What’s the problem, Brendan?”

"Are you on speaker phone down there," he asked.

"No," I replied.

"Abasi can you take this off speaker phone up here? I need to talk to Petrey privately."

Abasi pulled out the small jack plug and the speaker crackled off.

"Petrey, I am so sorry but I need a little time before I attempt to come down there, I should have mentioned it earlier but I am claustrophobic. I thought I would be OK after all this time but I am not."

"That's OK, Brendan, you just stay up there close to the phone in case we need anything."

"I need to explain something to you, Petrey. When I was a little boy of about five I was playing in my Grandmother's house and I got locked in her old oak trunk. I was locked in there terrified for about 5 hours before I was found and when I was found I was shaking uncontrollably and I had been sick everywhere inside the trunk."

"Brendan don't worry about it, it's OK."

"Petrey, I thought I had got over it but the second I saw the cage disappear I had to run outside and be violently sick. I told James and Thabo that it must have been something I had eaten. I just feel so stupid."

"Brendan, it really is not a problem, if you decide you would like to come down later then you can, in the meantime I am sure there are lots of things to do on the surface."

I switched off the phone and turned back into the cavern to explain to the rest of the team that Brendan was feeling unwell.

I now took time to have a good look at our surroundings. I think that maybe at an earlier stage in the history of the mine this had probably been at the bottom. The main chamber was huge and in places over 20 feet high and mostly 10 feet or more everywhere else. I paced it out and estimated it to be 140 yards long and about 20 yards wide. Along the walls there were heavy chisel marks where the miners had originally dug the ore out from the rock face.

Chris and Pieter had hung Kerosene lamps for several yards in each direction and we explored the rest of it with torches. At one end it seemed to taper off into nothing but at the other end several passages disappeared into the uninviting rock. Some of them opened up into small store rooms although there was nothing in them now. However a couple of them went deep into the hillside and right now we did not need to explore them as our priority was another 4000 feet or more down into the mine.

The one thing we did notice however was that it was extremely clean down here and there was little dust or debris lying around. Somehow I had an uneasy feeling about this damp and chilly mine with its eerie darting shadows.

Pieter and Rosa checked everywhere close to the cage and the shaft to make sure that the area was safe. Rosa notice that on the rear wall of the shaft away from our cage door were signs that heavy wires had worn away at the rock and caused quite a lot of damage. She said that if this had been a sustained action then it was quite possible that the wires of a previous cage could have become frayed and ultimately broken sending its passengers to their doom in the murky depths below. Rosa photographed the damaged rock which would eventually be added to the files that the government kept.

Whilst we had been exploring, Lisa had been taking notes; the lift had been going up and down bringing food supplies for us and Abasi kept up a running commentary from above.

At this stage we had no idea how long we would be in the mine as there was still a lot of work to be completed.

It was now time to go down to the bottom of the shaft and I opted to go down with Chris and Pieter. I felt that, as it was ultimately my operation, I should be at the forefront of this final stage.

Once again my stomach was turning over and an immense trepidation swept over me. Part of me wanted to go and see what had happened to my Uncle and all those other people who had perished but the other half hung like an awful dread of what we might find down there. Would we find rotted human remains or would creatures down there have devoured everything. It was a gruesome thought but also one we would have to face.

With my heart beating fast and loud in my breast and wet sticky hands we started the descent. Pieter had managed to rig up a torch in the centre of the cage which gave us limited light but also filled us with terrors as shifting shadows darted to and fro like ghosts and apparitions; coupled with our thoughts it was a terrifying ride.

After forty minutes we knew that the bottom must be close. We slowed the cage down in case there was a lot of debris so that we would not crash into it at any speed. Suddenly, the cage lurched sideways and there was a sickening crunch as we came to a sudden stop. We could not see what had happened but Chris, fearless as ever and carrying a torch in his teeth, climbed out of the cage and scrambled onto the top of it.

"There has been a bit of a rock fall," he called out to us, "and the cage has come to rest on a large piece of rock sticking out from the side of the shaft. From here it looks as if there is enough space to get past it but we will need to push the cage away from the side as we go down."

There were several of James's shoring planks in the cage and Pieter and I managed to push the cage away from the rock whilst Chris directed us. Inch by inch we traversed past the fallen rock. Fortunately the cable did not snag on the rock and Chris quickly rejoined us inside the cage. Once we started to descend once again I called Abasi on the telephone and explained to him what had happened.

The cage descended quietly for another 10 minutes or more, the silence down this far inside the ground was almost deafening and it was a relief when the cage ground to a halt.

The bottom of the shaft had been reached and we stepped out into the inky black cavern, a little over 8,000 feet down. The enormity of the depth suddenly struck me. We were over a mile and a half underground.

For a moment, which seemed like an eternity nobody moved and we tried to adjust our sight using only our torches for illumination. Light sand crackled underfoot as we moved into the mine.

Many coloured reflections bounced back like apparitions as torches picked out the cavern walls. The huge variety of different types of rock, limestone, chalk and thousands of different aggregates winked and blinked at us in the dancing torchlight.

But where were the bodies and the debris from the previous disasters? We could see nothing. It was so clean and tidy that it was almost clinical. As if the place had been swept clean. But by whom?

Pieter was baffled and said, “I have the charts for this mine and this should be where the disasters happened but there is nothing here.”

“Perhaps there was another shaft,” I suggested.

“Not according to this,” he said waving a bunch of papers in my direction.

I almost laughed and said nervously, “Perhaps somebody sent the cleaners in.”

I don’t think Pieter was in a humorous frame of mind because he just grunted.

The cavern was absolutely enormous and similar in shape to its counterpart at 4,000 feet; however this was much bigger. Strange unidentifiable noises reverberated and echoes could be heard bouncing through the empty, ghostly passageways.

Pieter insisted that mine shafts were always noisy because of water movement, rock-falls and often the scampering of small animals. These sounds were often magnified by their confinement in a huge acoustic auditorium.

Chris volunteered to go back up in the cage and act as guide to bring the rest of the team down. It would need expertise each time the lift went up and down to negotiate it around the rock fall.

Pieter suggested that Abasi send us down a wire strop and some pitons to drive into the shaft wall. This would pull the shaft cable close into the wall away from the fallen rock and hopefully avoid any further snags. Pieter and I waited until we heard Chris shout down to us that he was clear and proceeding up to the rest of the team.

I carried a small Digital Measuring Device with me and was able to quite accurately measure the height of the mine and also the width. However, the length would have to be paced out. Pieter said that the chart details that he had should be quite accurate although no digital device had been used when the mine was operational.

The height was measured as 71 feet and 2 inches and the width was 141 feet. This compared with the chart measurements of 70 feet and 138 feet. The chart was quite accurate. We started to measure up the length of the mine which Pieter said should be 2,085 feet.

As we moved through the passageway we continued to be astounded at the cleanliness of the mine and also the lack of any equipment. As each 100 feet was completed I marked the floor with big white cross using a box of chalks that I had brought specifically for this job.

I placed the mark at 1,045 feet which should have been the end but the mine continued on for another 40 feet or more. This was quite a deviation from the distance shown on the chart.

The cavern also opened out more at this end of the mine and there were many passageways leading away from the chamber. Pieter said it would be better to wait for more of our team to arrive before exploring further. We returned to the shaft end of the chamber to await our team.

It was a long time before we finally heard the noise of the cage returning. Chris came out with Lisa and explained that he had managed to wire the cable to the side wall and the cage was now running smoothly past the obstacle. It had been three and a half hours since Chris departed.

It was long past midnight but of course down here it was impossible to gauge the time. Chris, Mukesh and Lisa had brought food, water and sleeping bags with them and we made the decision to halt proceedings for the night. Jimmy and Rosa were to remain at the first level until the morning and the rest of us would bed down for the night here.

As I drifted off to sleep I was beset with many thoughts of what could have happened here. Where were Uncle Carl and his colleagues and where were the other lost miners. I imagined so many different things. Had animals dragged them all away, had the Himba managed to get to the bottom and empty it, or was there any truth in the legend of the Himba and their belief in their dead ancestors?,

I must have fallen asleep and imagined I heard noises coming from the passageways at the far end of the cavern. Although I slept, my head was filled with demons and ghostly thoughts and I awoke in the morning, once again filled with apprehension.

Whilst we prepared breakfast Rosa and Jimmy came down to join us.

Chris broke the ice and said “Did anyone hear any strange noises last night or was it my overactive imagination.”

“No it was not your imagination, I thought I heard something too,” I replied.

“I didn’t hear anything,” chimed in Pieter. “I slept like a baby all night until I heard you all moving around this morning,” he continued. “I think I could have slept all day.”

Mukesh said he did not hear anything. Lisa had disappeared off to find somewhere private to attend to her ablutions so did not join in the conversation.

We ate a hearty breakfast of meat and biscuits and washed it down with a cup of murky looking tea. It was no five-star hotel, that's for sure. I was almost embarrassed for Mukesh and Lisa because I am sure they had never had to rough it like this before but neither of them ever offered any words of complaint.

Lisa had found a small stream running through a tiny room just off the main cavern and commented on how warm the water was.

"I imagined the water would be quite cold down here," she said, "but it really is quite warm."

We were all ready to start exploring and we split up into three teams: Chris and Lisa, Pieter and Rosa, and finally, Mukesh, Jimmy and me. I rummaged in my bag and brought out three Acme Thunderer referee's whistles.

"These are only to be used in an emergency," I told them. "Can you also make sure that you all have enough sticks of chalk and ensure that you mark the walls with arrows every twenty feet or so. If the tunnel that you are in diverges then mark the way that you went very clearly."

In high spirits we all set off to explore and try and find answers to the hundreds of questions that needed answering. The most important ones being.........

Where were the bodies?
Where was the equipment?
Why was it so clean down here?
And more importantly, who had been here?

We checked our watches and agreed to be back in the main cavern in two and a half hours.

Jimmy led the way for our team and we were all armed with torches and extra batteries. We took the first passage on the right that appeared in the cavern wall just a few yards from where we were sleeping. After about twenty yards the ceiling of the passage became a lot lower and at times we had to stoop to get through. There were small cavities off to the side and they looked almost as if they could have been rooms of some sort. There were also signs of somebody having been there. It was not as clinically cleaned up as the main cavern. There were odd articles of clothing but these were quite small and would not have fitted any of our team. They were almost childlike. The material was not recognisable and seemed to have sheen on it and have a metallic finish. It appeared very durable and there were no signs of wear and tear.

There were also a number of utensils with a sharp point at one end and a scoop shape at the other not too dissimilar to a spoon. There was also a collection of metallic looking oblong pots that could have been used for baking.

Jimmy suggested that this might have been inhabited by African people because he had seen things like this in a museum in Cairo. However he couldn't remember what was said about them during his visit.

We found little else apart from a few items that looked a bit like medallions or buttons. These were also made of metal. I placed all the items that we found into my rucksack for further investigation later on when we met up with the other two teams.

Soon after this the passageway seemed to peter out, although at the very end of the passage there was a deep trough of water. We could not see the bottom of the water and there were no sticks available to probe it so I tied a small rock to a piece of string and lowered it into the water. It seemed to come to rest at about fourteen feet and I moved it around and it went no further down.

Just as we were about to depart from the trough, several large bubbles burst on the surface of the water.

Jimmy said, "I have seen this sort of thing up in the caves high up on Kilimanjaro. There must be an air source somewhere coming into the trough and it looks to me like this could be a sump."

"What is a sump," asked Mukesh.

"It often means that the cave system continues the other side of the water," replied Jimmy. "To access it we would need diving equipment. The wall probably goes down a few feet and then it has a gap at the bottom and you can move through and come up the other side into more passageways or another cavern. There are many of these sumps all over the world in cave systems. It looks as if the mine was adjoining a natural labyrinth of caves."

"There is nothing we can do now." I said. "That probably explains why there was diving equipment found by the Himba in the stores when they reached the 4,000 feet level."

"We have been down here for over ninety minutes and need to make our way back to meet the others." Mukesh interrupted.

After making sure that we hadn't missed anything we made our way back to the main cavern.

We could hear the other two teams talking excitedly long before we joined them. Both of them had tales to tell and I had to shush them up so that we could find out what had happened.

Pieter and Rosa had gone a long way down the main passage before finding a doorway with a metal door frame leading through into another passageway. Pieter said that the doorframe was quite safe at the moment but that it had rusted through considerably and would not survive too much longer. They also found old small gauge steel tracks that must have been used to transport the precious metals along to the main chamber. These must have been from a much earlier era because they were heavily rusted as were several hulks of the carriages that had once used these tracks.

They had found some artefacts similar to the ones we had found but they had also found about twenty metal sheets about ten inches square. Were these dinner plates? We placed the entire collection of artefacts together ready to transfer to the surface.

We called Abasi to see if everything was alright and he said that Brendan wanted to speak to us.

"Brendan" he shouted, "Petrey is on the phone,"

Brendan seemed much more relaxed and calmer now, and asked if Chris would come up and collect him. Chris was quickly in the cage and on his way.

Lisa said that she and Chris had followed a route that had brought them to a dead end and so they retraced their steps and found another passageway. When they had gone only about twenty-five feet they came across a doorway that had been blocked off and nearby was another. She said it was really odd because the doors looked as if they were new and there was no sign of aging or rust at all.

Also around the bottom of the door there was a lot of moisture but it was not coming from under it.

We waited for Chris and Brendan to join us and we brewed a cup of tea whilst waiting and enjoyed one of our tasteless ration pack biscuits with our tea. I often wondered why ration packs were always made with the most awful tasting foods that they could find. We shouldn't have complained as Chris and Jimmy had brought them with them from the Kenya Navy base in Nairobi.

Brendan arrived and was looking very drawn and pale. Apparently Chris had kept him laughing all the way down with stories and anecdotes to keep his mind off the trip down. Nevertheless, he still looked very agitated. Very soon Brendan had relaxed and listened intently to all the things that had happened since our arrival.

I was extremely keen to retrace Lisa and Chris's steps and find these strange doors. They were exactly as they had described and did indeed look like new doors. There was something very familiar about the metal that they were made out of but I couldn't quite remember what it was.

Pieter set about trying to open one of the doors but it was totally impregnable. Chris called Abasi and asked him to send down explosives. Whilst we waited we tried the other door which did not appear to be as well fitting as the first door. After a little persuasion the second door opened a little and we were able to force it open wide enough for Lisa to struggle through.

It was a strange room and had unusual storage units. Lisa said she had seen nothing like them anywhere. She photographed the room thoroughly and searched every inch of the place. There was also a box that appeared to have files inside. It was extremely heavy and took Lisa all her strength to drag it to the entrance.

We then assisted her back out through the door and then pulled the strange filing cabinets through as well.

Before there was time to study what Lisa had found, the explosives had arrived from the surface. Pieter and Jimmy placed the charges around the first door and then we all evacuated the area. Once we were clear Pieter pressed the plunger and there was a huge explosion and a cloud of dust permeated the air.

When we returned to the door something inexplicable had happened or should I say not happened, there was not a mark on the door and no damage whatsoever. What type of metal could withstand a huge blast of dynamite? Then it dawned on me where I had seen the metal before. It was in the North Atlantic and those same samples that had been sent to Emio in Washington.

What was this stuff and where had it come from? We had far too many questions about this project and so far we had no answers.

I had a flash of inspiration and said to Pieter, “What if we place the charges around the door in the solid rock, do you think we could get the door open that way.”

“It’s worth a try,” said Pieter.

After two more large explosions the door fell in. There was still no damage to the door but it was of no importance because we now had access.

We rushed into the empty space beyond the doorway in time to hear a lot of noise and scurrying further along the passage. Chris said he was sure he caught sight of something moving very quickly away from us. He said it moved at amazing speed and he was unable to follow it.

Nothing ever seemed to faze Chris; however he seemed quite shaken up by what he had seen. He said he was convinced that he had seen at least two forms moving rapidly along the passage and that they had looked quite human albeit smaller, almost child size.

After the dust cleared we all moved as quickly as we could along the passageway following the creatures that Chris had seen. After two hours of searching we had found nothing. Then without warning there was a huge explosion and an immense force nearly blew us off our feet with shrapnel and dust being propelled towards us with great velocity. I think we all sustained various cuts and scrapes from the flying debris. We remained with our backs towards the explosion with our hands over our heads trying to protect ourselves for a number of minutes.

Whatever had been in the mine was now never going to be found. The rock fall following the explosion was huge and completely sealed the passage. Several times I had thought that maybe some of the local African inhabitants might have been responsible for the strange phenomena that had occurred. But I no longer believed that because they would not have had this sort of technology. Whatever had happened here was the work of highly intellectual beings, but right now I had no clue as to who they might have been.

Pieter and Rosa wanted to go back to the surface and get government forces to come and search the area. They were of the opinion that this was probably the work of terrorists using the mine as a hide out or headquarters. I doubted that and after Pieter and Rosa had left for the surface we discussed the events of the day.

Since the explosion we had completely forgotten about the files that Lisa had brought out with her. Now was a good time to look at them. The file carrier seemed to contain about a dozen strange looking charts but we were unable to decipher them. Brendan said he had never seen a language like it. Mukesh said it certainly wasn't Sanskrit and I knew that it wasn't a western language.

Pieter called us later to say that a helicopter had been despatched to scour the surrounding countryside and that about thirty troops were being sent to the area. They were going to remain on the surface and brief the helicopter pilot on what they thought was going on. I knew he was way off track but I did not have a credible explanation for what had happened or what had been seen deep below the earth's surface.

Although the writing could not be deciphered the charts themselves looked very similar to any other chart. Brendan scoured each one very carefully and spent several hours before he suddenly became very excited.

"Petrey, Just look at this, what does it look like to you?"

I looked but could not recognise anything at all.

"I think this is a chart of the North Atlantic," he said. "Look this is Iceland, and here look, Greenland, and over here looks like the coast of Norway. This could be island of Surtsey and this could be the Northern Irish coast and right over there could be the Canadian coast."

"You could be right," I said, "But why would there be a map of that area in a file down here?"

Brendan laughed and said, "I have no idea."

I explained to the others what Brendan appeared to have found whilst they continued exploring the local area. Brendan continued to pore over the maps and charts. After another hour or more I heard him shout,

"I think I have found something else."

I left what I was doing and went back and stood behind him.

"What is it?" I asked him.

"Look at this, Petrey, this looks like a star chart and if I am not mistaken this looks like the star Sirius."

I had to agree with him there were definitely similarities.

I was not sure what else we could achieve down there but perhaps further searching would uncover more secrets that would give us a clue as to what had happened to all those who had disappeared.

It was getting late and the time had passed quickly. Mukesh thought it was time to call it a day and have something to eat. We packed all the files back into their strange container and placed it by the entrance to the lift shaft. Our pile of artefacts was quite considerable but we still did not know what they all were.

It had been a long day and we were worn out, so after a hearty meal we settled down for the night. Our sleeping bags were all close together and we carried on chatting about the strange day until one by one we drifted off to sleep.

I had nightmares all night and I dreamt of all sorts of ghoulish things. I imagined creatures creeping up on me in the oily dark of this subterranean crypt. I must have eventually gone into a deep sleep because the next thing I remember was Lisa screaming. I scrambled out of my sleeping bag and ran over to Lisa. She had stopped screaming but was emitting heart rending sobs and she was trembling violently.

“Whatever is the matter?” I asked her.

“Look,” she said, “Look over there.”

It was very dark so I lifted my torch and aimed it in the direction that she was pointing. Standing just a few yards away I thought I saw a small strange looking creature. I stared at it in astonishment and abject fear. By now the rest of the team were awake and making a lot of noise trying to work out what was happening.

I was frozen to the spot; the creature was about four foot six inches tall. It had an elongated head, broad shoulders and a slim waist with long legs.

As my terror eased I became aware that this creature had not moved. The darkness had played tricks on my vision and with the torch movement it had seemed animated.

I approached the creature and it still did not move. As I crept closer I could see that it was solid and was little more than a statue, albeit a very odd one. However, more to the point, how did it get here?

I felt the statue and it was extremely cold to the touch, almost as if it was made of solid ice.

By now everyone was fully awake; Lisa had calmed down and Mukesh was comforting her. Chris and Jimmy started searching the area to see if there was anything else amiss. I tried to lift the statue and found that it was not only cold but also exceedingly heavy. I managed to lay it down on its back so that I could explore it more thoroughly.

In the bottom of the base there was a hollow compartment and nestling inside was a piece of parchment. It was like papyrus but felt oily. It was stuck and it took a little effort to free it from the confines of the cavity. I finally had it in my hands and took it back to where Lisa was now looking more relaxed.

"Are you feeling better now?" I asked her.

"Yes, I'm sorry I screamed but it terrified me and I thought it was alive."

"I am not surprised it scared me too," I grinned sheepishly.

"What is it, Petrey, where did it come from?"

"I have no idea, Lisa; perhaps this parchment will give us more clues."

I carefully unfolded the parchment and lying inside was a plain piece of white paper. I quickly turned it over and to my total surprise there was writing on it. I turned it round and read the following:

Petrey,

John Bainbridge
Peter Hawkes
Carl Jonesy

All of us named above are alive and well and living a rather strange existence. Paul Driver was sadly killed trying to escape from them. I cannot give you any details except I have befriended one of them and it is he who has delivered this to you. I am desperately hoping you find this letter.

We will all remain alive as long as their existence remains secure.

They are brutal and without conscience and have only kept us alive so that they can learn all about us. Escape is not a possibility and they will kill without remorse it they believe their identity could be compromised.

Get out of the mine as quickly as possible or live to regret it.

THEY ARE WATCHING YOU

Carl Jonesy.

The blood had drained from me and I felt totally sapped of all energy and just collapsed. My torch fell from my grasp and smashed on the floor of the mine. It was several minutes before I regained my strength and managed to sit up. Chris helped me to my feet and led me back to my sleeping bag. Lisa had recovered quickly and came and sat next to me.

"Are you alright," she whispered. "What was in the letter?"

I put my fingers to my lips and just said, "Shhh."

Mukesh was holding the letter and looked stunned as he finished reading it. Without a word he put his fingers to his lips and passed it to Chris.

After a cup of tea I felt my senses returning and I began to recover from the shock. I think even Chris had been affected by it. We all sat together and talked very quietly. The idea that Uncle Carl was not dead had never entered my mind.

I asked Chris what he thought that we should do.

"Do you want to go back to the surface immediately or shall we stay and see if we can find out any more about whom or what is going on here?"

Lisa looked at me for guidance and then said, "If Mukesh and Petrey want to stay down here then I will too."

We jointly made the decision to carry on our search throughout the rest of the day and then try and get some sleep and return to the surface on the following morning.

I returned to where we had blown the door off and tried to retrieve some samples. Although the substance was extremely hard I did manage to get a small amount of material that I hoped I would be able to test. Jimmy and Chris went off to search other passageways but Mukesh and Lisa stayed close to me.

Chris found some more charts in another room close to where we found the first ones. We all looked over these charts but nothing was apparent so we placed them in the container with the others to be studied in daylight.

Jimmy became frustrated and vented his wrath by shouting, “Why don’t you come out and show yourselves instead of hiding away in dark corners.”

There was no response but I think he felt better for getting it off his chest. Jimmy was usually so quiet and reserved but I imagine under pressure everyone acts differently. He was soon back to his usual cheery self.

Later on he joked, “I don’t know what I expected but all this crap is so frustrating. Who are these people?”

We eventually tired of exploring and sent a message to Abasi to send down more meat for our evening meal. By the time it arrived it was getting very late; we were all feeling hungry and tried to enjoy the food. Thabo had been into the village and got some fresh fruit and this came down with the meat.

I joked with the team, “This is like a five star hotel with all this good meat and fresh fruit, all we need now is a bathroom en-suite and large fluffy bath towels.”

I had tried to lighten things up a little but I don’t think it worked because there were some very serious faces at the end of our meal.

I asked that whoever woke up first in the morning should wake the rest of us and we would start to evacuate the mine as early as possible. I had no idea what the night was going to bring!

There was very little talk as we settled down for the night and I can only imagine that everyone was still feeling shaken at the terrifying events of the day.

It was very quiet and soon I heard Lisa snoring gently next to me. Chris and Jimmy were whispering and Mukesh was tossing and turning in his sleeping bag. Brendan was writing notes by the light of his torch.

Then the night of terror began! One minute it was quiet and then there was a noise like a gentle wind blowing down the passageways, strange sounds echoing off the walls that quickly turned into a shrieking roaring sound that felt like a hurricane coming at us. We were all instantly awake and fearing for our lives. Lisa clung onto me and the others still in their sleeping bags sat with their backs to the wall of the mine huddling together to escape the onslaught. Then as if by magic, the strange looking plates and buttons that we had found earlier, our bags and all of our water and food supplies were sucked up to head level and starting flying dangerously around the chamber in all different directions at once.

We dived for cover behind anything that would offer protection. Then appeared these ugly terrifying apparitions who resembled the statue that we had found; only these were much more deformed and grotesque and they zoomed right up to us so that we could smell their putrefying breath before they zoomed away again. They kept up this barrage of abuse for what seemed like hours but was probably much less. Then all went quiet for several minutes and we thought the onslaught was over.

Up until this point most of what had happened was pure fright but what happened next was very much more than that.

Our Kerosene lamps blew out and our torches died leaving us in the cold, chilling, and pitch black of the mine. Lisa screamed and was brutally torn from my grip and I had no idea where she was. We were being attacked by forces with incredible inhuman strength and we had no idea what was doing the attacking. Close by Brendan squealed and I heard what sounded like a body slumping forcibly to the ground, there was the gut rending sound of bones being broken and I could hear Chris swearing and then his speech was cut short as something must have struck him in the chest and his breath just whooshed out of his pain-wracked body.

Then came that chilling wind again that blew me into the nearby wall of the mine and rendered me senseless for several minutes. Next I was blasted by heavy articles that I can only imagine were the contents of our bags and the items that we had found. I dropped onto all fours in an effort to find Lisa and tried to call her name but the cruel wind that seemed endless ripped the noise away from my mouth and rendered my efforts into silence. I found a body at my feet and although I couldn't see or hear who it was, I knew they were in terrible pain.

The onslaught was still not over because the storm force winds increased and it felt like a hurricane as boulders, rocks, gritty sand and other debris tore through the mine with an enormous velocity leaving us all even more bloodied and torn.

I have never been so terrified and I had difficulty in controlling my bodily functions as I thought we were all going to die as had so many others in this deep dark unholy grave. What had I unleashed with my stupid plan of trying to find the cause of the accidents in the mine? What unworldly creatures were running amok and trying to brutally slaughter my friends and me. We were afraid for our mortal lives.

It was a horror that you cannot possibly imagine and when it was finally over we were torn, damaged, broken, exhausted and terrified. Whoever or whatever was doing this had the final word. In a loud crackling inhuman voice came the words, "GET OUT OR DIE."

This was followed by one final act of terror. A huge explosion collapsed all the passageways leading into the cavern and for many moments we could scarcely breathe as a huge pall of dust filled our eyes, ears and lungs with so much debris that we were left spluttering and choking on the ground.

Chris was the first to move and scrambled painfully amongst the carnage to find an unbroken lamp. He eventually found one and lit it and placed it on the ground just a few feet from where I was lying.

The scene before me was like something out of a horror movie and it took several minutes to force my body into some action.

Jimmy's leg was broken in two places and it was him who had been lying semi-conscious at my feet. Mukesh had a deep gash above his left eye that was bleeding profusely. Lisa had received a huge bump on the head and was lying about ten feet away and moaning as she regained consciousness. I rushed to her side to comfort her and make sure she was not mortally wounded.

The rest of us had sustained many lacerations and bruises all over our bodies and we were lucky to have survived the carnage that lay all around us. We hobbled and helped each other towards the cage.

Knowing that we could not all get in the cage at the same time. We sent Lisa, who was still not fully conscious, Mukesh, Jimmy and Chris up to 4,000 feet and told them to return the cage to us as soon as possible. Brendan, who had earlier been scared of coming into the mine at all, volunteered to stay with me and wait for the cage to return. Just before it left, with still violently trembling hands, I managed to throw the file carrier into the bottom of the cage.

After the cage had gone Brendan was violently sick and complained of a bruise behind his right ear. There was nothing to see in this shadowy half-light and I couldn't feel any injury to his head. I found a small protective alcove and I bundled Brendan into a sleeping bag to await the return of the cage. Fortunately for us there were no more incidents that night at the bottom of the mine.

It seemed like an eternity before the cage slowly bumped into sight and we gingerly left our sparse cover to hobble over to the cage. As I went I managed to grab a couple of the strange plates and some bits of clothing that now lay scattered across the floor of the mine before throwing myself into the cage behind Brendan. The next forty minutes or so seemed like hours before we finally reached the rest of the team at 4,000 feet.

Jimmy was sitting in a corner, his leg in a makeshift splint that Chris had put on him. Considering his ordeal he was bright and chirpy.

"When we have any injuries on Kilimanjaro," he laughed, "Chris always looks after the ladies better than he does the men."

"That's because they're better looking than the men," joked Chris. "Anyway you just like all this fuss; you're quite capable of fixing your own splint."

It was good to see this friendly bickering between these two lifelong pals. They were certainly good under pressure and were a huge morale booster for the team especially after all we had been through that night.

Brendan had done so well to overcome his fear and come down the mine but it was now starting to tell on him. He was nervous and tense and shaking violently and I needed to get him out as soon as possible.

I discussed it with Chris and we agreed the first to go would be Brendan, Lisa, Mukesh and Jimmy. Chris and I would tidy up down here and wait for the cage to return for us. We assisted Jimmy into the cage and made him as comfortable as possible. Whilst we waited for the cage to return Chris and I discussed the operation.

I said to Chris, "Did we achieve anything here or was it a complete waste of time?"

"Well, Petrey, it depends on you really."

"What do you mean, Chris?"

"If you walk away now after everything you have put into this project then it was a waste of time. If you go away, take a short break and then assess what has happened here and completely investigate all of the clues that you have and follow them through, then it was not a waste of time...Petrey, do you want me to be honest with you?"

"Yes, Chris, please."

"I don't see you as a quitter, Petrey, and I have taken a good look at your team, they are good people, they won't let you quit." he said with confidence, "I won't let you quit. Let's get away from this place and find somewhere quiet to relax and then get together in a quiet room and brain storm this thing. Petrey, if you would like Jimmy and me to go with you, then we will. We will support you all of the way."

"What about your commitment to the crown as a serving officer?"

Chris just smiled and said, "Why don't you let me worry about that?"

"Chris, do you think that Jimmy will still want to be involved after his awful injury?"

"Oh yes, I know Jimmy only too well, he will definitely want to be in on this."

"Thank you for your support and confidence in me, I'll try not to let you down."

"You won't, Petrey, you won't, I see the hunger in your eyes, and it's very rare."

Chapter 16
Recovering from the Ordeal

I was very keen to be away from the mine as quickly as possible and instructed Thabo to strike the camp. Thabo seemed a little upset that we were leaving so soon but then we hadn't really had a chance to fully debrief him. I wasn't totally sure what to tell him anyway. He asked if he could have a couple of hours off to go to the village and say goodbye to his local friends. We had been at the mine for just three days.

An odd thing happened, Chris went with Thabo to the village and I wondered why he had gone and how they would treat him or even if they would let him into their midst. They were gone for about three hours and came back from the village together talking animatedly.

Abasi started dismantling the lift motor and coiling the wires back up again ready to transport. He greased every single piece of the equipment and packed it away in the carrying cases. Pieter and Rosa had returned to Cape Town to make their report. Fortunately they were not aware of the previous night's terror and we had decided not to inform them. I am not sure that they would have believed us anyway.

Chris could speak a little of the Bantu language which was the language of the villagers and he wanted to ask them if they had seen or heard anything strange in or around the mine. He also asked the elders to speak to the Himba and ask them if they knew anything. He asked them to tell the Himba that we had left quite a lot of equipment and stores down at 4,000 feet and if they wished to have it then they could.

Chris thanked them for their help and hospitality and hoped they considered him to be their friend. He asked that should they find out anything then would they pass it on to Thabo who in turn would pass the information on to Jona-Baas. Chris also gave them the Talisman given to him by Mukesh and told them that it was from a great god from the East who would watch over them. They accepted it with great reverence and told him that he would be their friend always.

I don't know what happened to Brendan whilst we were down in that mine but he started acting strangely. I know he was claustrophobic but this was altogether something different. He became listless and moody, unlike him, and on several occasions said that we should forget the whole mission and go home. I had never seen this side of Brendan; he had always been so calm and sensible. I eventually shrugged it off and put it down to stress, although not before mentioning it to Chris who promised to keep an eye on him as well.

Jimmy remained cheerful and upbeat and Mukesh quickly recovered from his deep wound. Lisa also recovered but a little more slowly. She was very withdrawn for a few days before regaining her previous vigour and enthusiasm. Everyone apart from Brendan was well on the way to recovery. However, up until now none of us had discussed the dreadful events of that night down the mine.

James, Thabo and Abasi were a little more than curious but remained patient when we told them that once we had found a quiet venue to relax at for a few days then we would tell them everything.

With everything hastily packed we left the campsite and started our way back down the hills. We had several small mishaps on the way down and I began to wonder if our operation was being jinxed. However none of them were too serious.

A wheel came loose on the trailer which housed the cage and lift gear and very nearly came off. Fortunately Thabo noticed it and we averted another catastrophe. The water that we were carrying suddenly became contaminated and James and Lisa were violently sick for a few hours. Then a fallen tree blocked our way and we had to divert across a swollen stream and we became bogged down in the sodden soil.

Up until now Thabo's friends from the village had kept a very low profile and apart from Chris's extraordinary visit with them they had stayed aloof. However, when we became bogged down, about twenty young men and one elder suddenly appeared. With them all singing and chanting and in high spirits they attached ropes to the vehicles and one by one pulled us out of our watery bog.

As we drove away from our rescuers they were dancing and waving at us like young children. It seems that they were always there when we needed them and Thabo was very proud of them.

Fish Hoek was our next stop but John and Madoda were not in residence and had probably returned to the Caltex office in Cape Town.

It was a peaceful place to stop and far enough away from the mine for everyone to relax a little. There was a crude bathroom and a tap with a shower fitment and Lisa asked if she could make use of it first. Who was going to argue with that suggestion, certainly not me? She emerged looking refreshed and happy. I think it was the first time she had smiled properly for several days. I wondered if our relationship would survive after all the disasters that had befallen us. Little did I know but she also feared the worst and worried in case I had changed my mind.

Whilst we all showered Thabo prepared a feast for us and we were soon feeling very much better. All except Brendan who remained in a melancholy mood and he did not join in with the conversation but slipped away to bed before everyone else.

In the night there was another mishap but fortunately Abasi had been sitting in his Land Rover when a fire broke out and destroyed Lisa's diary and a few other things of little importance. However, the loss of the diary was a blow to us. Lisa later confided in me that the destroyed diary was a hard copy and that she still had a complete set of her original scribbled notes and could reproduce the diary later on. I don't know why but I told her not to tell anyone else that she had notes.

I was beginning to wonder if we were being sabotaged but could not think who it could be or why, unless we were being stalked by whoever had been in the mine. I spoke to Thabo and Chris and told them of my worries. Chris said he was already wondering why there had been so many mishaps and was also suspicious.

"Have you told anyone else apart from me and Thabo about your concerns?" Chris asked.

"No, not a soul," I replied.

"For the time being say nothing, Thabo and I will keep our eyes open and try and find out what is going on."

It was good to relax at Fish Hoek and do nothing for a couple of days. Jimmy's leg needed to have some proper treatment so Chris and Mukesh went off in one of the Land Rovers to the nearest hospital. Thabo had given directions telling them there it was only a couple of miles away.

I asked Brendan if he wanted to go with them but he declined saying all he wanted to do was go home. I was very worried about him; it was so unlike him to act in this manner and I wondered what was bothering him. "Perhaps you will feel better when we get to Cape Town and if not then you can get on a plane and return to the UK," I suggested.

Jimmy was back in a couple of hours sporting a nice white plaster cast. Chris caught him chatting up two of the black nurses, they had signed his cast and also written down the telephone number of the hospital so that he could call them up.

"You'll get yourself into trouble Jimmy," Chris joked with him.

"They are looking for a good looking white husband and it looks like they couldn't find one and so you will have to do," he chuckled.

"Thanks Chris, I like you too," Jimmy replied.

That night I was fast asleep in my tent with Lisa sleeping peacefully in the sleeping bag next to mine. We had both discussed our concerns about our future together and I was feeling so much happier after she had declared that she was still very much in love with me and always would be.

Suddenly I felt someone touch my shoulder and jumped up with a start. It was Chris, who put his finger on my lip to keep me quiet.

"Someone is out there," he whispered.

"Thabo is circling round so that whoever it is will not escape."

"What have you seen?" I asked Chris.

"Someone in dark clothing is inside one of the Land Rovers, but I have no idea what he is doing."

"What shall we do?" I said to Chris. "What if he has a gun or a knife?"

"Well let's hope it is not as big as mine," said Chris producing a handgun.

We crept stealthily out of the tent and kept in the shadows and approached the Land Rover. There was someone just climbing out of the back carrying something under his arm. At that moment Thabo rushed in at a prearranged signal from Chris. Chris also ran in at the same time. Whoever it was dropped what he was carrying and sprinted into the dark shadows of the bush.

Chris picked up what the intruder had dropped and brought them into the light. It was the charts and maps that we had retrieved from the mine. It was too dark to chance following our strange intruder into the undergrowth and so we would have to wait until morning. Thabo said he would try and track whoever it was as soon as it was daylight.

Thabo set off at daybreak to track the mysterious intruder and was gone less than an hour.

"Jona-Baas, it is very strange. I followed the tracks out into the bush and found that someone had remained just a few yards away from here and then doubled back into the camp. There are too many footprints in the immediate vicinity for me to find out where they went."

"Does that mean they are going to try again," I suggested to Chris and Thabo.

"We will need to be very watchful from now on," said Chris.

Later that night someone released the handbrake on one of the rovers. They tried to push it over the rise where it would have crashed down through the bushes and onto the bank of the stream some 40 feet away down a sharp incline. Thabo managed to stop it before any damage was done but he did not get a chance to pursue the perpetrator because had he done so then the vehicle would surely have crashed. There was nothing in the Land Rover of any great value and I think it was done to try and create a diversion.

Later still, on the same evening, Thabo spotted someone creeping close to the vehicles again and tried to grab him. With incredible strength he hurled Thabo away and tried to escape. Chris and I were close by and we rapidly closed in on him and grabbed him from both sides. Again, with great strength and agility he shrugged us off and sprinted away, but not before Chris pulled a button off his dark jacket.

The whole situation was becoming dire and whoever was doing this must have been very brave or very stupid, or both. Sooner or later he must realise that he would be caught.

Chris handed me the button which was more like a toggle and was the sort that is used on an outdoor mountain or hiking jacket. I had seen one very similar to it lying in the back of one of the Land Rovers several days before but had no idea who it belonged to.

I thought it was time that we told the rest of the team that we had become the target of a vandal or madman and to keep their eyes open and report if they saw anything suspicious at all. Brendan just muttered, and said that none of this would have happened if we had gone straight home. I really was getting quite concerned about his health and wondered if I should get him away from there.

When we got up the following day Brendan could hardly walk and he complained of pains in his arms and chest. I was now very worried and thought we had better get him to a hospital in Cape Town as quickly as possible. We had already decided that we needed to move on and Cape Town was as good as anywhere to have a rest and also mull over all of the things that had happened and research all the items that we had found.

It was less than twenty miles into Cape Town and we were there in a little over thirty minutes. Thabo lead the way and took us directly to the hospital.

Groote Schuur Hospital is a large, government-funded, teaching hospital situated on the slopes of Devil's Peak in the city of Cape Town. This was the hospital where the first successful human heart transplant was carried out by Doctor Christiaan Barnard in 1967.

Brendan was admitted and given a private ward where tests were started on him immediately. Whilst we sat in the waiting room Abasi came into the room carrying a black coat.

“I just found this in the back of my Land Rover,” he said, “And look, there is a button missing.”

Before we had time to discuss it any further, the doctor came out of the ward to see us.

“Good afternoon, I am Doctor Darvall.”

"Tell me what Professor Crickley has been doing recently," the Doctor asked.

We explained to him about our expedition to the mine but did not divulge too many details.

"Why do you ask, Doctor?" I queried.

"Well his body seems to have undergone massive trauma caused by an excessive amount of physical exercise." He replied.

"Also his mental state is below par and he is barely talking and when he does he is incoherent."

"I thought at first he might have had a heart attack or stroke but his internal health is exceedingly good and I can find no explanation for his current condition."

"Can I go in and see him Doctor," I asked.

"You can but I have given him a sedative to help him relax, he will probably sleep for about twenty-four hours."

"Thank you, Doctor."

Chris and I went in to see Brendan but he was sound asleep.

We returned to the car park where our Land Rovers were lined up like a military convoy.

Thabo was looking puzzled and said, "Jona, I don't wish to upset you but that black jacket with the missing button belongs to Brendan."

"How could that be?" I stated not expecting and answer from anyone.

Jimmy piped in, “You know, Petrey, Brendan has been acting very strangely for the past few days, do you think he might have something else wrong with him?”

“Like what,” I said a little too shortly. I immediately apologised. “Sorry, Jimmy, I didn’t mean to be rude.”

Jimmy continued, “I don’t want to alarm you but sometimes people who get a tumour often have a complete change of character and become like someone completely different. Didn’t you say that Brendan had a pain behind his right ear?”

“I did but that was immediately after that horrific attack down in the mine. I thought he must have picked up an injury there.”

“It would be a good idea to mention it to the Doc and get him to check it out.” said Chris, and he wandered off to see if he could find Brendan’s doctor.

Whilst he was gone Thabo had been busy trying to find a place for us to camp for the night. Behind the hospital was a huge meadow and this land also belonged to the hospital and apart from a few domesticated cows there was nothing else there. Mukesh took Lisa and they went off to find the administration office to explain our situation and enquire if we could camp there for a couple of days. They came back with thumbs up.

Thabo, Abasi and James moved the Land Rovers onto the meadow and started unloading the tents. One or two of the guy ropes had started to fray and so Jimmy found himself a comfortable spot and set about splicing some more ropes for the tents. His leg was getting more comfortable but he complained of it itching inside the cast.

Chris located the Doctor and told him about the pain that Brendan had mentioned behind his right ear. The Doctor promised to investigate as soon as Brendan had slept.

At about eleven o'clock the following morning the Doctor came over to our makeshift campsite to tell us that Brendan was fully awake and that he had carried out a physical examination of his head and indeed there was a small swelling behind the right ear. The nursing staff were taking blood tests and swabs and he hoped to have more conclusive results within the next few hours.

In the meantime we thought it was time that we had a complete wash-up of all the events to date. Thabo, James and Abasi has still not been fully debriefed about the events in the mine that dreadful night and I was wondering how to put it across to them without sounding completely nuts. I then smiled ruefully and thought, well if they think I'm nuts then there is a whole bunch of us.

Neither Thabo nor Abasi had any difficulty in understanding the situation. However, James was a lot more sceptical but realised that with so many reliable witnesses something really strange must have happened.

"So what now," James asked.

"I think we will have to examine all the evidence that is available and also try and decipher the maps and charts that we brought out. The same charts that someone was very keen to get their hands on. Before we go any further with this discussion does anyone want to opt out of any further activities?"

Abasi said that he had a wife and young son back in Kenya and although he would like to be involved he would need a little time. I assured him that it would probably be several months before we would attempt anything else and that Mukesh, Lisa and I would need to return to India for business reasons.

I had other reasons for returning to India; one that was very important which required me attending a wedding. But those were personal reasons and it was not necessary for me to mention them now.

Doctor Darvall came to see us later on in the day and was looking very puzzled. “My staff and I have carried out lots of tests on the Professor and oddly enough we cannot find anything medically wrong with him. He continues to be vague about everything and keeps saying that he would like to go home.”

“Doctor, how do you explain the lump behind his ear?”

“At the moment, I cannot,” he replied. “I have taken a biopsy and that is the only result that I am waiting for. I should have the results of the biopsy within the hour and I will keep you informed of anything we find.”

The Doctor returned as promised within the hour and asked Chris and me to accompany him to his surgery.

“I have brought you to my office because of what I have found, and I am not quite sure how to approach this subject. I suppose I had better get straight to the point; your friend has been chipped.”

“What do you mean by chipped Doctor?” Chris asked him.

“The lump behind Brendan’s ear is some sort of computer chip similar to the sort that you put in dogs and cats.”

I was dumbfounded and could not comprehend why Brendan would have a chip behind his ear.

I recovered quickly and asked, “Doctor, can this be removed without causing too much pain or any long term effect?”

“I am not used to seeing humans chipped but in animals they can be inserted or removed with no trauma whatsoever so I think my answer would be yes, it can be removed.”

I looked at Chris for him to indicate that he agreed with me and he nodded and said, “In that case Doctor would you be able to remove it for us?”

“It is a very simple procedure. My staff nurse can take it out, I will ask her to do it for you. Do you wish to be there for the procedure?”

“Yes please, Doctor, I am sure he would want his friends there with him.”

“In that case Mr Jonesy we will do it immediately, come along.”

Brendan was still looking serious and acted quite morose when we entered the ward. The Doctor had a chat with him and said he would like to take a sample from behind his ear for further tests. He thought it better not to tell him that a chip was being removed.

The staff nurse came in and asked Brendan to turn onto his left side. She swabbed the area with an antiseptic liquid and then removed a scalpel from a sterile box.

In less than a minute she placed a minute metal object into the palm of my hand. As she removed it Brendan lapsed into a deep sleep which lasted about ten minutes. He came round very slowly and then looked around as if trying to adjust to his surroundings.

“Hi, Petrey, Chris. Where am I and why am I here? Was I hurt? Will I be able to come back into the mine with you?”

Chris looked at me and shrugged.

"How are you feeling Brendan," I asked him.

"I feel fine," he replied, "What is going on?"

The colour had returned to Brendan's face and he looked so much better. Chris and I asked him a few questions and he just laughed and said, "What is this? Twenty questions."

Brendan seemed to be perfectly normal and was back to his usual self. He remembered nothing since that awful night in the mine and had no recollection of events since them. He did say that his arms and legs were aching but the way he had fought us off and run away it was not surprising.

We thanked the Doctor and his nursing staff and took Brendan back to our camp in the nearby meadow.

We quickly filled in the gaps in Brendan's memory and then tried to figure out what had happened. Whilst we were being attacked in the mine someone or something had inserted this computer chip into Brendan's neck and since then they had been controlling him. We think that they had been responsible for all of the sabotage attacks on us and also the charts by using Brendan. It was a chilling thought that they could have so much control.

That evening we had our last meeting and meal all together. It would be many months before we reconvened on a different continent for the final conclusion.

Thabo was very upset that we were splitting up so soon and made me promise him again that I would be in contact with him soon. Jimmy was unable to drive so Abasi took his place behind the wheel and late the following morning we set off back to Johannesburg.

Chris was very keen to be involved with our future endeavours and said he would be very happy to travel to the UK or India, and in the meantime, he would get Jimmy back to full health.

Mukesh had taken a back seat and been a valuable team member whilst we had been away but now his leadership returned and he took control of events. He made a promise that he would continue to be involved and also fund the operation until its conclusion. To my surprise, without any prompting from me, he offered James a job in Delhi. James said he was available immediately as he had no close family in the UK.

I was worried about Brendan returning to the UK on his own and asked Mukesh to invite him to come with us for a couple of weeks recuperation. I also believed it would be valuable to have him in India as we investigated our artefacts and charts.

Mukesh smiled at me and said, “Petrey you are so pushy. I intended inviting Brendan anyway, don’t be so impatient. I also have a feeling that you might need him very soon for another project.” He winked at Brendan.

Was I being dumb, had I missed something? I made no further comment.

I glanced at Lisa who appeared to have a smile on her face and her face coloured up as our eyes met.

Chapter 17 New Plans

We bade farewell to Chris, Jimmy, Thabo and Abasi at the airport and boarded a plane to Delhi. Poor Thabo looked so hang dog as we departed and I felt sorry for him. He had loved being with us was completely at ease in our company.

Our flight took us by South African Airways to Mumbai and then on to Delhi on Jet Airways and a flight time of nearly seventeen hours.

On arrival back in Delhi I installed James and Brendan in my apartment and Lisa insisted that I move temporarily into her apartment until permanent accommodation could be found for James.

Brendan had now fully recovered from his ordeal and was now even more determined to find out what had happened. Mukesh had a team of chemists and physicists working for him in his petro-chemical department and put them at our disposal. They would test all the samples and also take a look at chip that had been put into Brendan's neck.

Whilst Brendan worked with the samples, I set about finding a cryptologist to help us to decipher the maps and charts. I also contacted the Indian National Cartographic Association based in Hyderabad to see if they would assist us.

Mukesh gave us the use of a large room where we could all work together on our project. Within a week this makeshift laboratory was a bustle of activity. We had a couple of scientists, a cryptologist and a cartographer. Then there was Brendan, Lisa, me and occasionally Mukesh.

I felt a little embarrassed about spending all my time on the project and spoke to Mukesh.

He just laughed and said, "If I need you to work I'll come and get you. Anyway for the time being James is doing some good work and learning the business very quickly. I must thank you for bringing him to work with us; he is a conscientious and industrious professional and fits in well with the team."

The cryptologist took photographs of every inch of all the charts and fed the details into their vast database to see if there was any correlation with anything they already had.

The cartographer pulled up dozens of maps and tried to match them up with current maps of the world.

It was several days before either team had any breakthrough at all. The cryptologist said that he had some fairly positive results but needed to double check them because the results seemed highly unlikely. He eventually conceded his first findings and instincts and said quite simply, "Sumeria!"

He followed it up by showing me an article that he pulled up on his laptop.

During the 5th millennium BC a people known as the Ubaidians established settlements in the region known later as Sumer; these settlements gradually developed into the chief Sumerian cities, namely Adab, Eridu, Isin, Kish, Kullab, Lagash, Larsa, Nippur, and Ur. Several centuries later, as the Ubaidian settlers prospered, Semites from Syrian and Arabian deserts began to infiltrate, both as peaceful immigrants and as raiders in quest of booty. After about 3250 BC, another people migrated from its homeland, located probably northeast of Mesopotamia, and began to intermarry with the native population. The newcomers, who became known as Sumerians, spoke an agglutinative language unrelated apparently to any other known language.

In the centuries that followed the immigration of the Sumerians, the country grew rich and powerful. Art and architecture, crafts, and religious and ethical thought flourished. The Sumerian language became the prevailing speech of the land, and the people here developed the cuneiform script, a system of writing on clay. This script was to become the basic means of written communication throughout the Middle East for about 2000 years.

"The language on your charts appears to be very similar to the early language of the Sumerians. The Sumerians lived in the area by the Tigris and Euphrates Rivers now called Iraq.

"Now that I have identified the language it should not take too long to actually decipher the writings on the charts. I have a computer programme that will do much of the work for me."

The cartographer found a number of strange marked positions on the charts and at first they seemed random positions but after a great deal of research and getting hold of some geographical maps with pinpoint grid references and the use of Google Maps he was able to ascertain that several of the marked positions were those of the deepest recorded caves in the world. There were other marked points and they marked other extensive cave systems.

He handed me a list of the points he had identified. They were in order of depth starting with the deepest.

1. *Krubera-Voronja Cave deepest known cave 7,188 feet in Georgia on the Black Sea*
2. *Illuzia-Snezhnaja-Mezhonnogo Two times larger than the world's deepest cave also in Georgia*
3. *Gouffre Mirolda France*
4. *Vogelshacht and Lamprechtsofen, Salzburg, Austria*
5. *Reseau Jean Bernard, French Alps in Samoëns*
6. *Torca del Cerro del Cuevon, Located in the Picos de Europa mountains in the northern coast of the country*
7. *Sarma, Georgia*
8. *Shakta Vjacheslav Pantjukhina, Georgia*
9. *Sima de la Cornisa - Torca Magali, Spain*
10. *Cehi 2, on the Italian Slovenia border*

Other places marked were caves in Iceland, Norway, Canada and an underground system about which little is known in the North Atlantic and underwater in the relatively new island of Surtsey. (A little over a hundred years old, appearing in 1963 and continued growing until 1967.)

"I also managed to retrieve the following short report from our office's mainframe."

LAVA CAVES IN SURTSEY

The Surtsey lavas are of alkali basaltic composition and because of their low viscosity they tended to flow in tubes and closed trenches,

especially from the western lava crater where the lavas formed a 100m thick shield. Although lava caves were discovered by visitors at least as early as 1966, the speleology of Surtsey did not really attract the attention of scientists until recently, when two members of the Icelandic Speleological Society visited Surtsey to investigate the lava caves. In addition to two lava caves recorded by Olafsson (1982), eight new lava caves were investigated. Most of the caves are emptied sub-horizontal lava tubes; others are emptied near vertical lava feeder channels in the eastern lava craters. The composition is still very volatile and it may be some considerable time before scientists can full explore the huge cave systems below Surtsey.

"The markings on the chart somehow show this to be of significant importance to whoever marked them.

"Once your cryptologist has finished his work, I am sure you will have a much clearer picture of the purpose of these charts.

"I think my work here is finished and, if so, I would like to return to my offices. If there is anything that crops up later then please, contact me and I will endeavour to assist you again."

Brendan quietly said to the cartographer, "We have no idea what we are dealing with here and so we would all appreciate a high degree of integrity."

"Don't worry. We are duty bound to keep all of our clients' secrets totally confidential." With that said, he was gone.

Lisa and I were starting to spend a lot more time together and with me installed in her apartment, albeit temporarily, it really gave us an opportunity to get to know each other better. We had so many of the same interests; classical music, the theatre, dancing, although I have to profess to being a real amateur in that field. We also enjoyed quiet intimate dinners, although Mukesh often gatecrashed these events but we really didn't mind. I was beginning to see that my future life would be spent in India.

Lisa took me to so many places to enjoy India's culture. The languages, religions, dance, music, architecture, food and customs differ from place to place within the country, but nevertheless possess a commonality.

India is the only country in the world to have so many religions and beliefs. The culture of India is an amalgamation of these diverse sub-cultures spread all over the Indian subcontinent, and traditions that are several millennia old. It was such a fascinating place and I couldn't get enough of it or Lisa. She had captured my heart.

We started to talk about marriage but I saw so many obstacles in the way.

Lisa said to me, "I love you and there are no obstacles."

But I knew there were many and I was frightened of them.

We were both from totally different cultures and backgrounds and I knew we needed to face them. She came from a hugely privileged background and I from the middle classes. I didn't want people to think that I was marrying her for her money, but I knew they would. She dismissed them all saying that other people's views were not important and that love conquers all. I wished I could believe her.

Finally the Cryptologist was ready for us and what told us was difficult to comprehend. No, it blew our minds.

It was Saturday 13th December 2087 when we all sat round the boardroom table with the cryptologist standing at the head of the table setting up his multi-media equipment. James, Brendan, Lisa, Mukesh and I sat quietly waiting for him to begin.

"Good morning gentlemen," he began, "Oh, sorry, and Lady. I think this is going to be a very long day and I have a huge amount of material to cover. Perhaps it would be prudent to stop for a coffee and biological break about every one and a half hours if you are all in agreement."

We all nodded our assent to that suggestion.

"I need to set the scene for the charts and so I hope you will bear with me if I tell you a rather long story."

He began, "All of you here have had a reasonable education and some of this may not be entirely new to you but have any of you ever heard of the 'ANNUNAKI'?" He brought the word up onto the screen. We had all heard the word but none of us was really au fait with it.

"The records about them appear in Sumeria about 3,000 years ago.
They came from another planet
They were particularly interested in gold."

He now had our full attention as he brought each line up onto the screen.

"It is firmly believed by the Sumerians that the Annunaki were on Earth about 450,000 years ago, primarily looking for gold, which was very important in their culture, and perhaps for their longevity.

"Not surprisingly, such advanced beings in ships and with 'magical' technology were viewed as gods. The main person was Anu, in charge overall, probably remaining in orbit around Earth.

"Beneath him were Ninhursag, Enlil (brother and sister) and Enki, as well as Marduk, Inanna and a variety of minor deities each with their own areas of responsibility. The following is indicative of the education they brought with them.

"This advanced culture seemingly sprang up overnight. It bore the hallmarks of an aware and technologically capable society at a time when no-one can point to any possible precursor. Taxes, irrigation, public buildings, priesthood, a civil code, factories, all appeared pretty much out of nowhere.

"And what of the strange fixation we have with adornments, precious metals and sex? If the records are exact, then these same traits were those of the aliens. They taught the Sumerians well."

We discussed each facet of the information and tried to digest the meaning of it all. Some of it we had heard about before but it was all a fairy tale with no hint of reality to it at all, or was it?

Coffee and biscuits were brought round at regular intervals whilst discussions continued, somewhat heated at times.

"Now that I have put all of this before you, I need to try and explain what I have discovered on these charts."

Once again he switched on the multi-media projector and in big letters the words

'BATTLE PLAN" appeared.

"I believe what you have here is an intended Battle Plan."

There was total silence for a few moments as we tried to digest what he was saying.

"Do you think that they're they going to attack Earth?" Brendan asked seriously.

"No, if I have translated this correctly I think it is an internal battle between two factions of the Annunaki. I think that some of the places marked on the charts are currently housing a peaceful faction of them and these other beings whoever they are wish to destroy them.

"If I am correct then there are about 4,000 of the peaceful contingent living beneath the surface of the earth somewhere in the region of Iceland.

"Let's call the others the 'aggressors', who I think are inhabiting the caves in and around Georgia.

"It appears that most of the European caves are somehow interlinked at a level below that which is shown on earth charts. From my calculations I estimate there are about 6,000 'aggressors' living beneath Georgia.

"They have been coming to and from their planet for many generations but every 3,600 years a lot more immigrants arrive as their planet moves closer to earth. The time for the next close pass is very soon and the "aggressors" wish to make room for more of their own sect and wish to dislodge the other peaceful clan."

We were totally stunned at what he was telling us and it would have been easy to dismiss it all as a huge prank, but we had close up experience of the horrific power and hate of these attackers. We had suffered at their hands down the mine in South Africa.

I was about to ask a question when I realised I knew the answer. I was going to ask why had they been in a South African gold mine, of course the cryptologist had told us that they were 'particularly interested in gold'.

"Do the charts indicate when this attack will take place," I asked.

"They intend to destroy their victims by April 2090, being ninety days before the next batch of immigrants arrive from their planet."

"Then we have about two years to find the peaceful Annunaki and warn them of their impending doom," said Mukesh.

Our two scientists had made some startling discoveries of their own. None of the products that we had given them conformed to any known substance on earth. By now we were almost certain that we were dealing with something extra-terrestrial.

Chapter 18 A Very Special Day

January 14th 2088,

Lisa and I had a quiet wedding surrounded only by close family and friends. Mukesh had given Lisa away and Brendan was my best man. Grace had flown out from London to be Lisa's maid of honour and two of Mukesh and Lisa's nieces aged four and five were the flower girls. My parents also came, postponing their planned trip to Israel by a few days.

It was a beautiful day and we were blessed with a cloudless sky. The wedding had been carried out in two formats, a Hindu wedding followed by a Christian wedding. Lisa looked absolutely stunning in her Victorian style white dress with a delicate lace shawl. Grace and the two little bridesmaids were wearing identical dresses in light primrose.

Mukesh, Brendan and I wore traditional morning suits.

Mukesh had borrowed a friend's house for the day and a beautiful white marquee had been erected in the garden. Greco Roman statues adorned the marquee and grape vines festooned the supports. The simple cotton napkins had a cameo picture of Lisa and me in one corner, something we would keep and treasure.

It was a stunning setting and our wedding reception completed the most wonderful day of my life. Mukesh had one more surprise for us, he had arranged for a private plane to jet us off to the Maldives for five days honeymoon. He said that he would have made it longer but he needed me back at the office to start earning my keep.

The beautiful sunshine, golden sands and the most beautiful girl on the planet completed an idyllic honeymoon and we relaxed away from the rest of the world for our few days away.

On return to Delhi, there was a lot of work to be done on our joint venture with Caltex only this time I was working for Mukesh.

For the time being the Annunaki would have to wait but we did have two years before it became urgent.

Mukesh was completely tireless when it came to work and he would often work very long hours and seven days a week to complete a project. Two more ventures were agreed with Caltex and I found myself doing tests on more potential oil fields. I spent a week off the South Korean coast and a further two weeks south west of Sri Lanka in the Indian Ocean.

Normal life went on but in the back of our minds was the nagging thought that we needed to arrange to go and conclude our business in the North Atlantic.

Lisa and I bought a modest detached house just south of Delhi and we enjoyed getting it ready for us to occupy with a small flower garden at the rear. I had roses brought in from the UK and they flourished in the warm weather. I always remembered my Grandmother's garden and in her memory I managed to get some honeysuckle to adorn the rear wall of the house.

We trawled round the shops and stores looking at curtains, drapes, lounge furniture and beds. We had been married a little over twelve months when Lisa broke the news; she was pregnant and we were both very excited at the thought of becoming parents.

Mukesh bought us a beautiful crib for the baby; it was a miniature four poster bed with pretty lacy drapes all round. He kept it at his apartment until the baby was born.

Time sped by very quickly and the oil business was thriving. However we were all becoming aware that we needed to start making plans to take a team up to Surtsey and see if you we could prevent a massacre.

Brendan had been back in Aberdeen for over a year now and was waiting for Mukesh and me to contact him. Fortunately, he had fully recovered from the trauma of having the computer chip inserted whilst in South Africa and he was ready and eager to embark on this new project.

He had also been in touch with all of our sponsors and explained to them that we had been to bottom of the mine and that nearly all the remains from the accidents had been devoured by animals and bugs.

They were all disappointed not to get any more from their efforts but I believe Brendan managed to spin them enough of a story to satisfy them.

Mukesh said that he needed to continue working but could now release me to fully concentrate on getting the team back together. Chris and Jimmy were still keen to come with us and they had both visited Lisa and me in our new home. I had briefed them on our findings with the maps and charts and what we needed to do next.

Jimmy's leg was fully healed and he was raring to go.

Getting to Surtsey was going to take a lot of planning because of its isolated location. We needed to obtain a boat that was capable of withstanding the winter seas in the North Atlantic. We also had to decide on whether we would need a submersible or if we could access the cave system using conventional diving equipment.

Chris, Jimmy, James and I were experienced amateur divers but Mukesh and Brendan were not. Lisa would not be coming with us this time because she would be getting close to her confinement and I did not want to jeopardise her health or that of the baby.

James still had contacts within the Royal Navy and we needed a diving team to go and assess how difficult it would be getting into the cave system from the water. Although the access would be under water we knew that the caves once accessed would be dry; after all there were a lot of beings allegedly living down there.

Grace had recently completed a sub-aqua course which would be of great value to her as a forensic geologist. Brendan gave his consent for her to join us for this operation.

April 2nd 2089

It was a warm spring day when James and I flew to Ireland and met Brendan in Londonderry. We booked ourselves into the Tower Hotel which is the only hotel within Derry's historic city walls. We had no idea how long we would stay but bed and breakfast was all we needed because the rest of the days would be spent trying to locate a ship that we could put to our use.

Londonderry Port at Lisahally is a port near Derry, Northern Ireland. It is the United Kingdom's most westerly port and has capacity for 30,000 ton vessels, as well as accepting cruise ships. It is situated on the east bank of the River Foyle at the southern end of

Loch Foyle, beside the small village of Strathfoyle. It is operated by the Londonderry Port and Harbour Commissioners, whose former offices, just north of the city walls, are now a museum.

We went along to the Port offices to find out what ships might be available for our use. We explained that we were just doing a geographical and geological check on the still expanding Surtsey Island.

Chapter 19 Cap'n Joe and *Latis*

The port manager gave us details of a retired trawler man who had been forced out of business early because of the fishing quotas that have put many fishing boats out of action.

Cap'n Joe has been fishing these waters for over forty years, man and boy. He started off with his father at only fourteen years old but had been sailing with him since he was about three years old.

We found Joe at a waterfront bar with a few of his old friends who had also had to take early retirement. I wondered what we were letting ourselves in for as we went in through the front door of the bar. Much to our surprise, Joe was not drinking but had a group of men, both old and young sitting in front of him and he was talking to them, or should I say giving them a presentation. We stood at the far side of the bar listening to him talking about what he knew best, the sea.

He was an engaging character and both old and young were hanging on his every word. As we listened he talked about different types of boat, mostly the older wooden types, he talked about clinker built boats and carvel built boats and the advantages of both and how they performed under different circumstances.

He talked about the history of each type, explaining how the first clinker build boats were constructed by the Vikings. He explained that the construction method is known in some places as lapstrake. It is a method whereby the planks overlap each other and make very strong and durable sea going vessels. In the early 19th century they also used this method with metal sheets for the then new steel boats.

We waited patiently and politely for him to take a break; in the meantime we enjoyed the landlady's recommendation of strong ground coffee and some of her home baked doughnuts.

At a little after 12 noon he brought the talk to an end and asked if anyone had any questions. There were one or two questions about weather conditions and recognising signs of bad weather. He then wished them all a safe journey home and asked them if they would like more presentations in the future. They all nodded in agreement and he said he would post the details with the landlady. Then one by one they shook his hands warmly and took their leave.

"Joe seems very popular," I said to the landlady.

"Very," she said. "What he doesn't know about boats and the sea isn't worth knowing."

"Are you here to see him on business?" she ventured.

"Not exactly, we are looking for someone with a boat and local knowledge of the sea and conditions," I told her.

"In that case you will not find a more competent man in the whole of Derry," she answered. "He is also loyal and dependable and would never let you down," she added.

Joe finished saying goodbye to his audience and sauntered over to the bar.

"Mary O'Hara, stop giving away all those delicious doughnuts to strangers when I haven't had any yet," he grinned at us.

"Have you come to see me?" he asked.

"Yes Joe, can we go and sit quietly somewhere as we may have a proposition for you if you are interested," I told him.

Brendan then added, "And we will pay you for your services."

"Ah, now there is a man talking my currency," he guffawed. "Come on let's sit over in the corner where we will not be disturbed and you can tell me all about your proposition."

James was the first one to start asking questions. "Is your boat a bottom trawler or mid-water trawler?" he asked.

"It's essentially a bottom trawler but it can do both," said Joe.

"How long is it and how many berths are there?" quizzed James.

"Stem to stern she is only fifty-two feet but a very good sea-boat that can endure the most arduous of weather conditions, and we can sleep fifteen people easily," he replied.

Brendan, James and I had discussed what we should tell Joe and decided to tell him that we were interested in exploring and charting the caves that had formed under Surtsey.

James wanted to know how long it was since she had been to sea and if she was in seaworthy condition.

"Well *Latis* (which means Goddess of Water and Beer) is an aging boat and the 'old girl' is not as good as she used to be so it might be wise to strengthen up one or two areas of her bottom but she is generally in good condition," he replied.

"I might be able to help there," said James, I am a shipwright by trade and spent thirty years helping the Royal Navy to keep its ships afloat, I don't know how they would have managed without me." He grinned.

The banter between us went on for most of the afternoon and at the end of it we shook hands with Cap'n Joe with a firm agreement that we would be very pleased to use his services. As an extra sweetener James agreed to survey the boat and repair and replace wherever necessary.

"She'll be good as new," quipped James jovially.

"I hope not," laughed Joe, "I had too many problems when she was new and had to bend her to my will."

"Well, I'll do my best not to incur the wrath of her skipper then," said James light-heartedly.

James agreed to meet up with Joe the following morning and go and take a good look at his boat. For the next couple of weeks James was in his element doing what he loved best, playing with wood and boats. He made a list of the things that needed doing but as an added extra he decided to strengthen the bows and double its thickness. This was just a precaution but in the high winds and the unpredictable weather in the North Atlantic he didn't want to take any chances of her getting severely damaged bows on the hard volcanic rocks of Surtsey.

Brendan and I needed to find out more about diving facilities and the best way to approach our access into the cave system within Surtsey. We were not professionals in this area and were only amateur sub-aqua divers and needed to talk to the experts about our expedition. We were both agreed that we would not divulge the real intentions of our dive but keep it to a simple exploration exercise.

James had recommended that we go and talk to an old friend of his, a Warrant Officer Mike (Bungy) Williams at Fort Bovisand on the South Devon coast just outside the Royal Naval town of Plymouth. He was responsible for running the Royal Navy Diving Centre and training Clearance Divers for operations around the world and often under the most arduous of conditions.

Unfortunately, James had to stay and finish work on *Latis* and so he sent his regards to Bungy with us as we flew off to Exeter Airport in Devon. An hour later and mug of tea in hand we were sat in Bungy William's office overlooking the beautiful blue of Plymouth Sound where we could see the Roscoff Ferry sailing slowly passed our position.

Chapter 20
Enlisting the Royal Navy

Bungy was a gregarious character that had served as a Royal Navy diver for over thirty years and had many tales to tell. We decided that it would be folly to try and get help from him without humouring him by listening to some of his sea stories. He was amusing and kept us spellbound with his stories for several hours. However he was also an experienced veteran of many diving experiences and it was worth sitting with him for this period. He insisted on entertaining us for lunch, after he assured us he could claim it back on his expenses.

Bungy took us in his car to the Mussel Inn at Down Thomas which was just a few minutes ride away. He told us that the pub served fresh seafood as well as steaks.

"Best pub in the area," he boasted. "Very old place built in the 14th century and has an infamous history of rum running and contraband. I sometimes wish I had lived in those times." He laughed. "Cheap rum, what more could you ask for?

"After all rum was the lifeblood of the Royal Navy many years ago." He added, "I don't know if you know anything about rum in the Royal Navy but up until July 1970 all serving men were issued with a rum tot every day. Shame, really and now nearly 120 years since it ended."

Bungy was doing most of the talking and we just enjoyed listening to this entertaining man. There would be time for us to tell him what we needed after lunch and I think he was enjoying having this diversion from his usual daily disciplined routine.

Lunch was truly delicious and both Brendan and I took the opportunity to enjoy a selection of local sea-foods. The platter was huge and we struggled to do justice to the scrumptious fare.

We were served six raw oysters on the half shell with ice, six raw Littleneck clams on the half shell, cooked lobster, and six cooked jumbo shrimp, peeled and de-veined, with tails on, cooked blue claw crabs, all with lemon wedges and mustard sauce.

Despite all the talk of rum, Bungy ate lunch sipping a glass of chilled sparkling water with a piece of lime. He chuckled, "I do like a tot of rum, but these days I usually only have one on special occasions, you know birthdays and anniversaries." He sighed ruefully.

Once we were back in his office he said, "Well I have bored you with all my old sailor blarney, now it's your turn. What exactly has James told you I can do for you?"

I explained to Bungy our plan to investigate the rock formations and also gain access to the cave complex below Surtsey in the North Atlantic. Bungy was well aware of the weather conditions and how quickly it could deteriorate. We explained that we would want to put a small team into the caves and that none of us were experienced divers. He considered it carefully for some time and asked quite a lot of searching questions.

Finally, after consulting his PC and making a couple of phone calls he said, "OK I think there is something we can do but you will have to give me a couple of days whilst I make further enquiries."

"What is your budget for this operation?" he queried.

"Give us a quote for the cost of this exercise and I will see if I can get approval for it." I told him.

"Come back and see me again at the end of the week and I will have a plan for you."

We shook his hand and promised to come back and see him on Friday. We had a couple of days to kill and decided to enjoy some of the local National Trust properties and beaches situated in that part of Devon.

It was about 11am on Friday when we returned to Bungy's office. He was not alone and had a youthful looking Lieutenant Commander with him. Bungy introduced him as the Assistant Diving Officer, John Christian, from the Defence Diving School based in Horsea, Portsmouth. We shook hands and he immediately went into his dialogue,

"The Defence Diving School is a Joint Service establishment. It was set up in 1995 from the Mine warfare and Diving Department at the School of Maritime Operations and the Royal Engineer Diving Establishment and formed in a purpose built facility based at Horsea Island following the closure of HMS Nelson, Gunwharf Site."

I think he must have quoted this many times before as he did it almost as if he was reading from a script. As soon as he had finished he relaxed and was all smiles.

"Bungy has told me of your requirements and I am sure we can help you. In a moment I will tell you what we can do for you but I need to give you an idea of costs before start. It will cost £100,000 plus a daily rate of £200 for however long it takes."

At this stage Bungy ordered coffee which gave me the opportunity to ring Mukesh and run the costs past him. I was a little worried that he might find it too much to continue but I needn't have worried; he sanctioned it immediately and asked that I call him later in the day and update him on our progress to date.

I wasted no time in informing John Christian that the plan was a go and the money was no problem and asked him for details.

"I am going to give you details of our submersible, the LR5, which will be phased out of operation due to new equipment that has been developed. This submersible has served the armed forces well for about 80 years and has had many updates and additions over the years. If I may say so it has been a fabulous tool and will be ideal for your needs.

"If I can give you a copy of the specification to read you will learn a lot more about its capabilities, bearing in mind that this is essentially a rescue vehicle but has been used for many other tasks."

The LR5 Submersible

The LR5 submersible is fitted with an integrated navigation and tracking outfit, developed by Kongsberg Simrad, which integrates the surface and subsea navigation data. The rescue coordinator on the mother ship uses the presentation from the navigation and tracking system and the images from the sonars and cameras to provide real-time detailed pictures of the distressed submarine and the deployed rescue systems.

The rescue submersible makes a watertight seal onto the distressed submarine's escape hatch. The watertight seal allows transfer of personnel without submitting them to the high external sea pressure. Technicians and medical officers can be transferred to the distressed submarine if required and survivors from the submarine are transferred onto the submersible.

Up to fifteen submarine survivors can be evacuated at a time to the mother ship or to a mother submarine. The LR5 could make up to eight trips to the distressed submarine (rescuing 120 survivors) before needing to recharge the battery power supply.

Portable decompression chambers installed on the mother ship are used to treat the survivors in order to avoid decompression problems. The survivors are returned to normal atmospheric pressure in controlled conditions and at a controlled rate.

The LR5 vehicle normally carries three submersible crew members, the pilot, a co-pilot and the systems operator.

The vehicle is equipped with a suite of tools including a Slingsby manipulator, an ejectable claw, secateur type rope cutters, guillotine action wire rope cutters and a 305mm disc cutter.

The communications suite on the vehicle consists of 10kHz and 27kHz underwater telephones, an acoustic pinger operating at 27.5kHz and a Model 2056 voice and pinger set, operating at 10kHz, 27kHz and 45kHz,

Operating conditions

The LR5 is capable of operating in sea-state conditions generating up to 5m wave height and surface visibility of at least 1nm. The LR5 two 6kW electric motors give a maximum speed of 2.5kt, which limits the rescue operations to conditions of a maximum 1.5kt seabed current and the maximum operating depth is 500m.

The LR5 has a 'cram capacity' of 15 at an internal pressure of five bar.

John Christian continued, "Now you have had a few minutes to digest the information, I will tell you how we can help you.

"First of all we can locate the cavity beneath the rocks that will allow you access into the tunnel system.

"Secondly with accurate use of all the tools that we have available in the LR5 we can create an entrance point and affix a seal onto it that will be compatible with the air lock fitted onto the submersible. If all goes well we can effect a completely dry entrance into the caves.

"However it is advisable that you still take all your diving equipment with you in case of emergencies. Are there any questions so far?"

"Just one question. How many of your personnel will accompany us for the operation?" Brendan asked

John smiled, “Well,” he replied, “you get me for starters; I’m your pilot, and then a co-pilot and a systems operator. The rest will be all yours.”

“Thank you, John, this offer of yours is better than anything we could have dreamed of,” I told him. “As you know we are adapting a fishing trawler so we will need you to send us details of adaptations we will need to do for the LR5 to operate effectively.”

“I will put the details together later on today and email them to you sometime tomorrow,” he answered.

“We accept your offer and I will put the request in writing and send it to you at Horsea along with all the dates and approximate time it will take.” I told him.

“Thank you both for your time and hospitality and I think we had better get back to James in Derry and make sure he is not building a new boat.”

Just as we were departing Bungy commented, “If you need an extra man to assist you then I would be willing to offer you my services free of charge. I will take some of the leave I have owing and would be delighted to be involved in a different project like this one.”

We were soon back in Derry after the short flight from Exeter and went straight to the dockside to see how James was getting on with his work. He hadn’t built a new boat but he had stripped out the stem post and was busy building a double post to fit in its place.

“I thought it better to build it all in one piece after finding some rot in the old stem., This way it will take a great deal of punishment if I build in some shock absorbers between the two stem posts.”

“How long will the work take?” I asked James.

"Now I have been able to assess it fully, there is probably a month's work here," he replied.

"When are you thinking of making the trip to the caves?" enquired James.

"Early in December, probably not the best time to be in the North Atlantic but we need to give these Annunaki a fighting chance of surviving," I answered.

"We have already seen the brutal side of their enemy and I hope we can prevent any bloodshed."

"If it is OK with Mukesh, and you, I would like to remain here in Derry for the next few months. I have spoken to Cap'n Joe and he is happy for me to remain aboard the *Latis* until we go. By the time you and the rest of the team arrive I will know the boat inside out and be aware of any foibles she may have."

Mukesh readily agreed to James's proposal of staying with the boat and thought it would be a good idea to have someone know the boat inside and out and also remain close to Cap'n Joe.

"The more James knows about the boat and conditions and how she performs the better. It may be vital to our success."

We wished James farewell for now and left the *Latis* in James's capable hands.

We spent half a day with Joe looking over charts of the area and also checking old weather statistics to assess what we might be letting ourselves in for out there in the middle of winter. We spoke to the local meteorological office and asked them if they could produce some long term indication of conditions and also if they could keep us updated by email. They agreed to send a weekly update.

For the time being our work in Derry was complete and it was time to go back to Brendan's house in Aberdeen and plan the rest of the operation. I sent John Christian a brief plan and said I would send him a more detailed timetable in a few weeks' time.

We arrived only three days before Grace was due back at University and Brendan apologised for being away whilst she was on vacation. She said it was alright as she had spent most of the time swotting up for her end of term exams and would not have been very sociable anyway. She was very excited about being invited on our trip to Surtsey which coincided with her Christmas vacation.

Brendan is a bit of a dark horse. I found out that he was seeing someone and he had never mentioned it. Grace, of course, knew about it and was extremely pleased for her father. Her name was Linda, and she was a physics teacher and a colleague of Brendan's. She is about two years younger and they seemed to have so much in common. I met her the day before Grace returned to London and we all went out for dinner, but not before I had called Lisa to let her know where I was and to find out if she was still in good health. She had to keep reminding me that she was pregnant and not ill.

Brendan prepared an email to send to all of the members of our team to ensure that we would all be available. We proposed a start date from Derry on the 4th December. Mukesh, of course, was the most important figure in our team considering he was sponsoring the whole operation. However, he said that he would make himself available on whatever date Brendan and I decided on.

December the 4th it was then, and we subsequently received replies from Jimmy and Chris confirming that they would be available for that date. I also had one sent to Bungy Williams, who replied immediately saying that his leave request had already been signed and he would be with us.

John Christian confirmed that the LR5 would be despatched to Northern Island at the beginning of December and would arrive by the 3rd in good time to be embarked.

Brendan had to contact Professor Julian Stubbs, Principal of Birkbeck University to ask if Grace could be released early for Christmas to come and work on a field project for a couple of weeks. He agreed in principle but asked Brendan to put it in writing and then he would approve it. He and Brendan were old friends and had studied at Cambridge at the same time.

Bungy gave us a call and said that he had secured an offer for us of a fifteen full sets of sub aqua equipment from Siebe Gorman, on loan for as long as we needed them. Siebe Gorman are the most prestigious company providing the very best equipment for divers for over 250 years.

Bungy was coming along for free and was already making his valuable presence felt. I realised how lucky we had been with so much support from so many people who were willing to give of their time and expertise for nothing.

The time went by very quickly; December 2089 was suddenly upon us and we were making our way to Derry. We booked into the Tower Hotel once again. Brendan and I arrived on the evening of the 1st December in advance of the rest of the team, to ensure that Cap'n Joe and James were ready for us. Over the next twenty-four hours Grace, Mukesh, Chris and Jimmy arrived. Early on the morning of the 3rd Bungy, John Christian and his co-pilot for the LR5, Barry Sheppard arrived on the dockside just half an hour before the LR5 arrived.

John and Barry spent the rest of the day loading and housing the LR5 onto *Latis*. They needed a welder to assist with the framework to hold it but this only took a couple of hours and the job was completed. Before nightfall on the 3rd December everything had been loaded and we were ready to go.

Mukesh insisted on us having a memorable evening before setting sail and he booked a table for nine in the hotel's award winning Walls Bar and Restaurant. He had also spoken to the Hotel Manager who had arranged for a local Irish Folk Group to come and play local music for us.

I don't know what it was but there was a feeling of pending doom in the air. We had a wonderful evening and both the food and the music were exceptional; however, it was all tinged with a strange feeling of some dreadful expectancy. Perhaps the memories of the mine in South Africa were still raw and I couldn't put them to the back of my mind.

What would we find out there and where would it end?

The following morning was windy, wet, cold and foggy and it was if the forces out there were going to try and keep us from leaving the safety of Derry harbour. Cap'n Jo was not fazed by it and said with a chuckle, "Oh, look, just a regular day in Derry, sometimes we get bad weather here."

A strong north easterly wind blew steadily as we made our way down Lough Foyle towards the North Atlantic. *Latis* pushed on hard as we approached the open ocean and she pitched quite heavily as Joe pushed her bows into the oncoming storm. Although she was slewing around quite considerably in the turbulent weather she was a strong stout ship that would take a lot more battering than this before sustaining any damage. However her crew were not in such a good state, and one or two were feeling the effects of 'mal de mare' and were looking a little green.

Even Chris, who had said he had done quite a lot of sailing, was very quiet and Mukesh who had never been to sea on such a small ship was looking very queasy.

Our headway was quite slow but by the following afternoon everyone but Mukesh had got their 'sea-legs'(ability to keep ones balance and not feel seasick when on board a moving ship). Grace astounded us all; the moving ship had no effect on her at all. She spent most of the time on the bridge chatting to Joe, who kept her entertained with many of his old sea stories. Joe even gave her the wheel and showed her how to steer by the compass without following the lubber's line.

We were making headway of about 10 knots per hour and our estimated time of arrival at Surtsey would be early morning on the 8th December, providing the weather did not deteriorate further.

John Christian used the time to brief us all about the LR5 and emergency escape procedures, should it become necessary. We all viewed the interior and became acquainted with the seating. Barry Sheppard allocated our seating positions and tasks that each of us would have to carry out on arrival at our destination.

John's plan was to lower the LR5 into the water and once we were clear of the ship he would turn on the underwater sonar system that would guide us to the right spot assisted by the Oceanic Global Positioning System that worked in conjunction with the sonar. It would find the spot with pin point accuracy.

On arrival John, Barry and Bungy would operate the tools to break through the surface rock and attach the water tight seal to the rocks directly over our intended entry. Weather permitting the operation should take no longer than about four hours to complete. The seal should then be left for about twelve hours to harden and then it would be ready for use.

We all then returned to the bridge.

Joe told us that many years previously there were about thirty-six different fish stocks in the North Atlantic including Atlantic cod and haddock, yellowtail and winter flounders, spiny dogfish, Atlantic herring, and less well-known species like blackbelly rosefish. Some of the species had been fished out but many more had moved northwards as the temperatures had increased over the preceding years. Each year the Atlantic was getting warmer and warmer as the ice at the pole was steadily retreating.

Early in the 21st century there had been a panic that the earth was creating global warming but it had been eventually decided that this warming was just a phase that the earth was going through.

The weather had not been good and we had a really bad squall on the night of the 6th and had been tossed around like a cork. However the morning of the 8th broke in bright sunshine; the sea had dropped and was almost flat calm. It is quite astonishing how quickly conditions can change.

Joe anchored the *Latis* in about five fathoms of water. The water was crystal clear and the bottom could easily be seen. It was craggy and much of it was covered in a yellow and green growth of seaweed.

We all gathered around the LR5 and as the winch lifted her over the side, we gently guided her with our hands to make sure that she did not crash into the ship's structure. When she was at deck level over the side, Bungy, John and Barry clambered aboard and then she was gently lowered into the water.

After completing his check list, John and his crew of two set off for the access point. They quickly submerged and the LR5 was soon lost from view. With luck she would reappear in about six hours. Fortunately the LR5 was fitted with the most up to date Gertrude (underwater digital telephone and integral camera system) available and therefore we were able to maintain contact with them at all times. Both ends were attached to a colour monitor so that we didn't need to interrupt any of their work and we could see and hear everything that was happening.

They quickly located the exact spot and set to work with the long retractable arm to clear away the debris and begin affixing the watertight hatch. They were in less than forty feet of water and so the visibility was exceptionally good. The only problem with volcanic rock is that some of it is very brittle and other parts are as hard as steel.

Most of the loose shale was quickly removed. The LR5 was hovering about 5 feet above the excavated area but now they needed to get in close and form a seal over the proposed break through spot. With precision accuracy John lowered the submersible to within twelve inches and maintained it at this level whilst Bungy and Barry lowered the waterproof skirt over the area. Filling the skirt with compressed air and using the LR5 to hold it in place they quickly broke through into the cave system below. Bungy then dropped through the hole and immediately affixed a seal to the underside of the hole.

The whole process took a little over three hours and, after making sure that there were no leaks, they ascended back to the surface and returned to the ship. The weather had so far been kind to us and we hoped it would continue for the rest of the operation.

It was now time to make plans but with very little knowledge of what we were up against it was going to be quite difficult.

I thought it only right that I should lead the way. The plan was that we would travel singly and with gaps of about 100 yards between each of us. Brendan would follow me and then Grace, Mukesh, James, Jimmy and Chris would bring up the rear. Bungy would remain at the entrance to the cave and both John and Barry would remain on the LR5 in readiness for a quick departure if necessary.

Chris and Jimmy both had firearms but Chris asked Jimmy to give his to me. Chris said that if I was leading the way then I should have some protection. I was extremely hesitant about carrying a weapon but then Chris reminded me of the horrors we had endured down the mine and said it would be better to be safe than sorry.

We would be entering the caves early in the evening and had no idea how long this operation was going to take us. We had no idea where these Annunaki might be, if indeed they were there at all.

I had brought the whistles with me that we had taken down the mine in South Africa and gave one to each member. "If there is an emergency of any kind then blow your whistle."

The weather had deteriorated a little by the time we were ready to start which made it quite difficult getting into the LR5. There was a lot of movement with it lurching and yawing and for a little time it was very unpleasant. As soon as Chris was aboard we battened down the hatches and submerged immediately. John wanted to get under the water fast and avoid being tossed around too much.

It was surprising how much room there was inside the craft. There was room for crew and up to fifteen others, so with only ten of us altogether it was extremely spacious.

It was very dark outside now but the LR5 was fitted with bright halogen underwater lights and so it seemed as bright as a summer's day. We were soon in situ above the entrance and John settled the craft above the hatch whilst Bungy went down to check that the seals were all working correctly.

He returned five minutes later with the thumbs up. So far, so good, I thought.

All of a sudden I had sudden surge of fear and I wondered if anyone else was feeling the same way. I looked at Brendan and realised he was going through the same emotions as me. He took a deep breath and grinned at me bravely.

Chapter 21
The Final journey

2015 8th December 2089

"Good luck everybody," I said sounding a lot braver than I felt. "This is it; this is what we have been working towards all these years. If we do come under attack or there is an emergency then Chris and Jimmy are the experts at this type of rescue and they will take care of evacuation and get us all back to the LR5 safely and as soon as possible. Are there any questions before we go?"

"Yes," said Grace, "I have a question. What happens if someone is injured and cannot walk?"

"Chris and Jimmy will take it in turns to carry a Neil Robertson stretcher in case of any such emergency."

It only took about fifteen minutes for us to exit the LR5 and assemble in the mouth of the cave. We were finally ready to go. We all had head lamps as well as torches and gave them all a final check before I gave the word for us to start traversing through the cave.

The first part of the cave was very wide with a high ceiling resembling a large auditorium but as we started on our way the path soon started to go downhill quite sharply, causing us all to slither and slide on the small broken stones that covered the surface. At times it was necessary to cling onto the algae covered damp rocks that formed the wall of this precarious pathway. The route we were following also started to narrow considerably and the ceiling got lower and lower.

Within less than ten minutes our progress was hampered with the roof now so low that we had to scramble through on our hands and knees, the small sharp volcanic particles penetrating my thick trousers and causing some discomfort as it broke the skin on my knees.

The others behind were at an advantage as they had the way lit for them by the person in front. That advantage did not last long because the tunnel then began a series of turns and bends plunging the followers into complete darkness.

Every one of us was now isolated and needing to find our own way through this dark and scary labyrinth. The torchlight formed shadowy monsters and demons in our fragile minds, causing heavy breathing and palpitations in us all as we fumbled deep underground.

Suddenly I could hear the roar of water and the walls of the passage and the floor were drenched. I shone the torch on the ceiling which was about seven feet high now, and I could see huge droplets of water dripping out of the dark grey porous rock. Round the next bend I could see the reason for all the noise as a torrent of turbulent water cascaded down through a huge misty cavern and then swiftly disappeared into a massive gaping crevice in the floor of the cave.

The sucking, gurgling sound it made was like that of a huge monsoon storm drain as thousands of gallons of water disappeared from view. I thought that this water would have come from a crack in the surface with a huge volume of water escaping from the North Atlantic Ocean. As I moved closer I could taste the mist as it filled every inch of this anchialine cave and I was surprised at how fresh the water tasted, only slightly salty.

I shone my torch all around the water feature and could see many different species of flora and fauna festooning every crevice. I would like to have stopped and spent more time but I was not here to enjoy the view.

Very soon I entered another large cavern and the passageway started sharply upwards. There were many small cavities along both sides and I was almost afraid to glance in their direction in case anything came rushing from them. Even so, I could hear the sound of small underground creatures scuttling to and fro. I guess I was becoming a little paranoid and my mind and imagination still held horrors from my previous encounter at the bottom of an African mine.

We had now been travelling for over two hours and so far there had been no sign of intelligent life, either human or alien. I stopped for a few minutes rest and to nibble on a chocolate bar and take a drink of water. Brendan, and then Grace, soon caught up with me and I checked that they were both alright before setting on my way again. I could tell that Brendan was not entirely comfortable, his claustrophobia was clearly showing but he made no fuss about it. It was traumatic enough for anyone being in this cave system but for Brendan it must have been a living hell.

I just patted him on the shoulder and moved off along the passageway again. There were a series of tunnels and passageways but I appeared to be following the main shaft and I tumbled into one cavern after another, steadily moving north-east.

I stopped suddenly. I thought I had heard something in the distance ahead of me and strained to see if I could hear it again. Then I heard it, a gentle shuffling sound just up ahead of me.

It was happening again, I started to tremble. Was I destined to be scared of my own shadow for ever? My stomach was churning over and I was feeling violently sick. I had to force my feet one step in front of the other as they tried to seize up and refuse to move.

Did I want to warn whatever was ahead of me or did I want to keep silent with the hope that they didn't know I was here. With huge grit and determination I forced myself on at a greater speed than before. I had made a decision; if it was going to be disastrous then I wanted it to be now and not later.

The shuffling noise continued but seemed to be maintaining the same distance from me. I called out to whatever it was and felt very foolish as I shouted, "Hello, is there anyone there?"

The shuffling noise ceased abruptly but there was no reply to my challenge. I moved forward again and this time almost at a run. I soon slowed down as a festoon of cobwebs hanging all across my route clung to my face and neck and I shuddered as a huge black spider scuttled away.

What other horrors did this cave hold? I thought.

I was entering another of the huge caverns; it angled upwards very sharply and I was slowed down by the acute incline. I looked up suddenly and something right at the top of the chamber moved quickly behind a rock.

A cold shudder coursed its way through my body and sheer terror controlled my very soul. My hands were shaking and I dropped my torch which shattered into hundreds of small pieces.

Up there on the rock was an awful figure so much like the grotesque statue we had seen in the mine.

At the same time my head lamp just fizzled out as if by black magic and I was left speechless and trembling in a cold dark tomb. I could hear sounds all round me; my fear was so great that I could no longer stand and crumpled onto the hard cold dark volcanic rock. My body lay convulsing and I retched.

I don't know if my mind was playing tricks but the memories of those putrid awful creatures zooming in on me seemed so real and I wondered if my ordeal would ever end. As I relived the terror of that awful night deep in the mine, a strong wind howled round me while I lay helpless and inert.

I wrapped my hands around my head, trying to protect myself, waiting for the onslaught of the missiles that would surely come, expecting that my body would be punished, abused, torn and bloodied again by these cruel creatures that were barbaric and merciless. Would I survive this time or was it time to die? I fumbled for the whistle in an effort to warn my friends but it fell from my trembling grasp and tinkled onto the floor to join the shards of my broken torch.

In what I imagined were my last moments I thought of Lisa and our baby and that I would never hold her in my arms again or ever see the child that we had made. Childhood memories flashed through my tormented mind: Mum and Dad; and my days at school - oh, why hadn't I worked harder at school; I was broken, screaming in terror and demented. Everything went black.

I vaguely recall being half lifted and dragged and more terrifying thoughts pierced my already addled brain. Where were they taking me, where were my friends, was I about to enter a hell where pain would rack my body for eternity?

As I slowly regained consciousness I realised I was not alone and a small creature was staring at me intently and I was aware that he was gently placing me in a comfortable position. It took several minutes for my eyes to focus and I was still shaking convulsively but almost resigned to whatever was going to happen to me.

Chapter 22 Meeting Regby

He would have been about five feet tall , powerfully built with bright green eyes and a shock of long blond hair, almost Nordic looking apart from his lack of height. He looked regal, terrifying, and majestic.

"Who are you"? I gasped in awe and fright. "Who are you"?

"What are you doing here?" I croaked.

He tilted his head to one side as if he was trying to understand what I was saying. It was right then that I was struck almost dumb for several minutes before I could get over the shock as I distinctly heard a voice say, "What do you want with us?"

Suddenly I was no longer frightened of this creature, his voice and manner showed no malevolence and he appeared quite nervous.

I repeated my question, my voice little more than a whisper.

"Who are you?"

He replied with what sounded like Regby Dornik.

"Regby Dornik?" I repeated and he just grunted.

After my gruelling, traumatic experience, I was exhausted and I slumped where I lay and fell into a deep sleep.

I don't know how long I slept but I slowly awoke and Regby was gone and I was wondering where my friends were.

I was overcome by emotion and felt close to tears and wondered if I had imagined the whole episode. I fiddled with my head lamp and miraculously the light came back on. I scrambled back towards the passageway from which I had emerged to try and find the rest of the team. Where were they?

I soon had my answer, there had been a rock-fall and I could hear voices and people scrabbling around close by. I called out and Chris answered.

"Petrey, are you alright?" he shouted.

"Yes, I am fine, are the rest of the team with you?" I called back.

"Yes, we are all here and unhurt but it will take some time to clear this fall."

"We heard you scream. What happened?" shouted Chris.

"I will tell you as soon as you get through this debris," I replied.

It took about an hour to clear away the debris from the fall and it made me wonder if this had been an accident or whether unseen hands had caused it.

Once the team was through we all scrambled into the spacious cavern where I had had my unusual and unique meeting with Regby.

He was nowhere to be seen and I quickly brought the team up to date with what had happened.

“Do you think that they are a threat to us?” asked Mukesh.

“They might be,” I replied, “but I am still alive and they had every opportunity to kill me or take me captive and they did neither.”

“Let us move forward slowly and carefully and see if we can make contact with them and make our intentions clear,” suggested Chris.

As we moved through this huge complex of caves we were aware that it was getting lighter and lighter and within minutes we were able to dispense with our lamps and torches. The murky shadows dissipated and we gained the impression of a light and airy warehouse.

Very soon we became aware that we were no longer alone and yet at this point we could see nothing or no one. It was just a strong feeling that we were being watched.

Then a gentle voice was heard echoing softly all around us; it was not chilling or frightening in any way and we stopped to listen,

“Petrey Jonesy and friends, come no further but tell us of your intentions towards us,” the gentle voice urged in broken English.

“We are here to warn you,” I stuttered.

Then he spoke to us again only much more clearly, and I could understand every word he said.

“Why have you come and how can you help us?” he said.

There was a noise about forty feet away and high up on a ledge in the cavern, Regby Dornik appeared.

The rest of my team who had not previously seen him were physically shocked and I could see and feel their fear.

Brendan just stood looking at him with his mouth wide open and his eyes transfixed in astonishment. He then stammered, "What are you?"

Regby's voice came clear and precise, "We are the Annunaki."

There was no movement from his lips. I turned to Brendan and said to him, "Did he just say that he was the Annunaki?"

"He did but I didn't see his lips move," replied Brendan.

Then it dawned on me, this creature was telepathic. He was talking directly to us and only Brendan and I could hear him. I asked him to repeat what he had said but make it audible to all of us.

He repeated for all to hear, "We are the Annunaki."

Then I noticed that he was no longer alone and other beings had come into sight. They kept a very low profile and remained hidden behind stalactites and stalagmites in the giant underground auditorium, watching him with ardent curiosity as he conversed with me. The striking feature about each of these Annunaki was that they all had green eyes and long blond hair. Although small in stature they commanded immediate attention because of their unusual features.

Then his lips moved and he started to talk to us verbally.

Regbie's articulation was unusual and I could not discern what sort of language he was speaking. I presumed that he was a male as

I had only glimpsed a few other members of the clan and they all seemed masculine in appearance. I made the assumption that if there were any females of this odd race then they were being carefully hidden, as were any children that they may have had.

Of course, there was no sky or real horizon in the cavernous hollow and therefore no indication of whether it was day or night, summer or winter, although the temperature seemed to be at a quite acceptable Mediterranean level, and the light that appeared to come from the rocks themselves was bright enough to fill every corner but not glaring or uncomfortable.

Considering our location that seemed most unusual.

Regby tried to talk to us all again but I was unable to comprehend what he was saying.

“Are you able to talk to all of us telepathically?” I asked him.

He nodded his head but spoke only to me again telepathically.

“What language are you speaking?” he asked

“English,” I replied.

“Wait one moment,” he commanded.

Grace came forward and said quietly to us. “I think he is talking in an old Sumerian language.”

“That is correct, Grace,” Regby interrupted in broken English, for all of us to hear. “I think I know enough English to talk to you verbally, but I may occasionally have to go back to telepathy if I am struggling to make myself understood.”

I then said to him, “We come as friends but we have chilling warning for you. There are others who would do you harm.”

Slowly more members of his clan came closer to investigate and we found ourselves surrounded by about thirty of his kind. It was a bizarre situation but we did not feel under any threat at all. They were not like the other Annunaki that we had encountered.

For about an hour we were individually bombarded by hundreds of questions but they were done telepathically and we were completely astounded by these friendly animated creatures who could talk directly into our heads.

Only Regby was able to speak any English and so their only method of communication had to be telepathically.

It was soon made clear to us that they had no contact with the rest of the human race and had been frightened that they would be treated as aggressive aliens and destroyed.

To make us more comfortable they invited us deeper into the cavern. Moving from the damp, rugged volcanic caves and into their domain was a complete culture shock. It was beyond belief.

We were invited into an expansive and very modern city underground. There were no vehicles but there were brightly lit streets with fully air conditioned homes. Everywhere was immaculate and we marvelled that this could all be happening under our very noses in the North Atlantic.

“Regby, how many of you live in here?” I asked him.

“About 4,000,” he replied.

“How is it that you are the only one who can speak any English?”

"I was selected as a young man to colonise this area and our leaders back on Nibiru or Planet X as you seem to call it encouraged me to learn the most prolific language on your planet."

"What was the point of learning our language if you were going to remain anonymous?" I asked him.

"It was in case by accident we encountered your species, and although we have tried to avoid that happening the unthinkable can happen, and of course it now has."

"So what is the purpose of your coming here in such great numbers?" I queried.

"Our planet is fraught with danger and our race is in peril of being annihilated," he answered.

"How and why?" I asked him.

"We have studied your culture for many millenniums," continued Regby in broken English. "And you have had many wars between many nations for thousands of years.

"Initially we did not want to come here, knowing of your history of wars and genocide. However, we are now in deadly peril on Nibiru. Our mortal enemies are now trying to completely eradicate our race of people."

"We have had dealings with your enemies, and have information that directly concerns your survival," I told him.

Regby resorted to talking to me telepathically again because he said he was struggling to keep up with me and needed to understand all the things I was telling him.

The reality of his telepathy suddenly hit me. Not only could he speak directly to me but he could also understand much of what I was thinking.

It was the first time I had seen him smile and he looked at me quizzically with his head at that strange angle that I soon recognised as being peculiar to him.

"Ah, I see you now understand," he said becoming more serious again. "I see your friends are becoming acquainted with my family. If you are willing, I would like to invite you into our history library which has a room big enough for us all to assemble and listen to your story.

"I believe you are a good man Petrey Jonesy and I am inclined to trust you and your friends, but we are still frightened of discovery by your authorities. Can you assure me that you will not divulge us or our whereabouts to them?"

"I cannot make promises for others, but I will ask them all for their joint agreement to your needs and requests," I answered him very seriously.

He must have spoken to the rest of the Annunaki who were conversing with our team because it suddenly went extremely quiet and they all moved silently towards a large well lit building about fifty yards away.

"Come Petrey, let us go and talk together," said Regby, gently prodding me in the direction of what I supposed must be the library.

Once inside we were surprised to see that the library was completely spherical inside and the centre of this auditorium was completely empty. Around the circular wall was what I thought looked like a huge plate rack which completely filled the walls. Apart from the entrance, there was an almost unbroken 360 degrees of these racks. On closer inspection I could see that the racks were completely full of strange metallic looking plates that I recognised from those we had encountered down in the mine.

Regby moved into a position where he could be seen by everyone. He nodded at us all and said, "Welcome to our new friends, let us make ourselves more comfortable and learn as much as we can from them and the warning they bring."

I think we were all wondering how we could possibly make ourselves comfortable in this totally void space that we were standing in.

Regby went on, "If you glance down at the floor you will see pairs of small box like shapes imprinted on it. Stand with one foot in each and get yourselves relaxed. My friends will demonstrate."

A series of popping sounds echoed around the empty auditorium as the Annunaki stood on the squares and, is if by magic, a cushioned stool appeared from the floor behind each one of them. We all followed their lead and within seconds we were all comfortably seated.

Regby welcomed us to the City of 'Babillu'. I immediately thought of the ancient city of Babylon and wondered about the connection.

For the next two and a half hours we were each invited to stand in the centre, which was in full view of all present, to give a detailed explanation of who each one of us were and why we were there in their underground city.

It was similar to being at one of our own presentations except that we were being monitored. There were a series of lights showing on a monitor hanging in the centre of the room. They were continuously blinking and I later discovered that they were able to assess if each one of us was completely truthful.

They became more than excited when Brendan stood up and explained how he had been tagged with a chip in his neck. They knew all about this technology but had never used it themselves. They believed it to be unethical and it clashed with their stringent integrity.

Whilst Mukesh was talking about the mine incident and the part he played in getting the Himba to believe he was a Herera there was the an intake of breath from many of the Annunaki; at the precise moment that the blinking lights increased in speed and intensity.

I could see that Regby was looking unhappy about something and asked him if there was a problem.

"It appears that Mukesh is telling lies about the episode of fooling the Himba."

"What makes you believe that?" I asked him.

Regby replied, "Our monitors indicated that his heartbeat increased and therefore he was not being truthful."

I tried to assure Regby that indeed Mukesh was telling the truth. It then dawned on me that Mukesh had always been embarrassed about dressing up to fool the Himba and that the thought of his deception had increased his heart rate. He was unused to deceiving people and felt uncomfortable about doing so.

I explained this to Regby who recognised that there could be truth in what I was saying.

They asked Mukesh to stand up again and Regby put a number of questions to him. On completion he said to Mukesh, "The Annunaki have to be sure that we are dealing with the truth; our survival depends on it. We apologise for our initial distrust and are now happy with your integrity."

"Mukesh looked at me sheepishly and said, "What did I do wrong?"

"It's alright, all is well," I answered him.

It was my turn again to stand up and talk to the Annunaki and I could feel my heartbeat increasing as I stood before them. I carefully retrieved the charts from my rucksack and held them in my hands.

I needed somewhere to lay out the charts and show them to Regby. He raised his hand and suddenly a large square table shot up out of the floor.

I laid out the charts and for several minutes Regby and just a few of his clan gathered around and peered intently at everything I had laid out. Although I could not hear anything it was obvious that they were conversing with each other. They looked visibly shocked and some of them were looking very distressed.

Regby finally broke the silence and asked, "How did you manage to decipher these documents which enabled you to come and warn us?"

I briefly explained to him that I was employed by Mukesh and that he had many experts at his disposal. We have some of the finest cryptographers and cartographers who were able to decipher and read these charts and documents.

"Why did you want to help us, Petrey Jonesy?"

I thought very carefully before answering him.

"After our terrifying experience down in the mine we could not allow these evil Annunaki to wreak havoc on other beings again.

"Mukesh has kindly used his own money to pay for the complete operation and as well as his generosity he is here offering to help in any way that he can."

"We are not warmongers, and have little idea of how to organise a defence against these very aggressive Annunaki so the only alternative we have is to flee and find somewhere else to create a new home."

"We are most grateful for your warning and would like to offer you our hospitality for a few days whilst we make plans for our urgent departure."

They were indeed great hosts and showed us round their compact modern city before giving us the banquet of a lifetime. The tables were laden with many fish and seafoods, some of which were familiar; however the vegetables were unique and none of us had ever seen anything like them.

They grew their vegetables under something that resembled glass cloches except they had an air conditioning system that gently forced damp air over the top of the growing vegetation which caused it to grow enough fresh food every day.

There was also a unique fish tank system that reproduced at an alarming rate. Over a period of eight days their complete stocks were replenished. We could learn a lot from this advanced race of friendly peaceful aliens.

Then they showed us the most amazing advanced technology we had ever seen. We returned to the library building where we had first shown them the charts.

Regby invited me to go and stand in front of a panel that had a number flashing lights.

“Petrey, state your name and your language and wait for a moment.”

I felt quite self-conscious talking to a panel of flashing lights but my inhibitions soon dissipated.

“Petrey Jonesy, English,” I stated.

There was a whirring sound that lasted just a few seconds and then a voice said, “Thank you, Petrey Jonesy, state your subject.”

I look inquisitively at Regby and asked him what I should do now.

“Just name a subject that you would like to know about and you will be guided to where you need to go.”

“Winston Churchill,” I stated.

There was a soft buzzing noise and a blue light was flashing on the far side of the room indicating one of the strange plates that appeared to be standing in a gigantic plate rack.

I walked over to the rack and picked up the plate that was being indicated. A voice then instructed, “Place the palm of your right hand in the centre of the plate and wait patiently.”

Less than two seconds later a metallic computerised voice stated:

"Sir Winston Leonard Spencer-Churchill, (30 November 1874 – 24 January 1965) was a British politician and statesman known for his leadership of the United Kingdom during the Second World War. He is widely regarded as one of the great wartime leaders and served as Prime Minister twice (1940–45 and 1051-55). A noted statesman and orator, Churchill was also an officer in the British Army, an historian, a writer, and an artist.

So far, he is the only British Prime Minister to have received the Nobel Prize in Literature, and he was the first person to be made an honorary citizen of the United States of America.

Churchill was born into the aristocratic family of the Dukes of Marlborough.

His father, Lord Randolph Churchill, was a charismatic politician who served as Chancellor of the Exchequer; his mother, Jenny Jerome, an American socialite. As a young army officer, he saw action in British India, the Sudan and the Second Boer War. He gained fame as a war correspondent and through books he wrote about his campaigns."

"Thank you, Petrey Jonesy, if you would like to learn more about your subject then please say 'MORE',", if not then just walk away from the library rack and the information talk will discontinue."

We were all stunned by this technology and Grace asked Regby how they had obtained all the information. He said simply that their advanced digital access facility could tap into any major computer systems in the world and this included libraries, museums, governments, military and many others.

"The system also contains a full inventory of all film and music ever recorded and could be accessed in same way.

"You are already aware of our telepathic ability and the library can be also used to receive information telepathically," he added. Also, the telepathy facility is a much better option because all knowledge received in this way will be stored in your brain and easily recalled. In other words, once received it will never be forgotten."

"For someone like you, Grace, who is still at a place of learning, this feature would be invaluable," he said with a gentle smile.

Everyone in the team had spent some time playing with this amazing technology and Brendan asked Regby and his team hundreds of questions and jotted down notes continuously. I could see that brilliant brain of his working overtime as he sought to understand how it all worked.

There was a hive of activity as Regby and his clan started the task of relocating to a new home. They pored over maps and charts trying to find a suitable place that would be safe from their enemies. They also made plans to leave a false trail hoping that they could lead the aggressor in the wrong direction.

This enormous upheaval was made even more difficult because they had to do it without anyone else on the planet knowing anything about it.

Then something completely unexpected happened that changed the course of their lives for ever.

Jimmy wanted to refill his water bottle and asked where he could get some fresh water. He had loosened the top of his bottle to pour away the few dregs that remained inside. What happened next was absolutely incredible. The bottle accidentally fell out of his hands and he dropped the bottle onto the floor. The remaining water was forced out of the bottle as it crashed onto the hard surface and two of the Annunaki standing nearby dived for cover.

Jimmy laughed and said, “Hey, it’s only water, it won’t explode.”

The two Annunaki looked visibly shocked and they backed away from him.

Jimmy told me about the incident and I immediately went to see Regby, wishing to explain to him what had happened. I half expected him to make light of it, but told him in case there were any repercussions.

“Oh no,” he uttered. “Your team must be more careful.”

I couldn’t understand and said to Regby, “It’s alright, it was only drinking water in the flask.”

“Yes, yes,” said Regby, looking positively shaken. “I don’t think you understand how serious this could have been. “Petrey you need to understand, water could kill us. Jimmy could have caused a fatality by his unintentional accident.

“The only water that we can tolerate has to be distilled. We suffer from a dangerous allergy to water and it can cause severe irritation of the eyes, nose and lungs and it also causes excessive burning of our skin. Ordinary water will incapacitate us, and often causes fatalities; salt water is even worse and is always fatal. Just a small splash of salt water will not only burn where it comes into contact with our skin, but it will quickly spread until it has consumed and burnt the skin of the complete body.”

“I am so sorry, Regby, we didn’t know.”

“How did you manage to get here as we are surrounded by the ocean?”

"Well for one thing we did not enter this cave system the way that you did. We came down from the surface to the North of the island. However, we did come in a submersible craft but everyone had to wear a water protection 'all in one suit'. To get us all here took many journeys as we only had 100 of these suits available when we arrived on your planet."

"I will brief the team about your condition and make sure that there are no accidents in future. There are people on Earth who suffer with the same allergy although it is probably not quite so severe. It is called Aquagenic Urticaria; however it is very rare."

I quickly found all of the team and asked them to go to the library as quickly as possible. I had stressed the urgency and within several minutes the team had assembled. Jimmy looked completely devastated when I told them of the Annunaki's dangerous allergy, but was relieved that none of them had actually been infected from his water bottle spill.

Before we left the library to continue helping the Annunaki to prepare for the evacuation, Brendan suddenly exclaimed, "Wait I have an idea. Where is Regby right now, I need to ask him a crucial question?"

Jimmy ran off to find Regby and within a few moments he returned with him.

"What is it?" Regby queried.

Brendan said to him seriously, "Regby, do all the Annunaki suffer with this awful water affliction?"

"Yes of course," replied Regby, "Why?"

"Perhaps you will not have to leave after all then," said Brendan.

The whole team was now gathered round Brendan, curious to hear what he had to say.

"What do you have in mind?" both Chris and I said in unison.

"I am not a tactician." said Brendan, "But why couldn't we protect Regby and his clan by using water to defend them from the enemy?"

For several minutes everyone was talking at once as they tried to get to grips with the implication of Brendan's suggestion.

Chris spoke loudly and firmly, "I think we need to sit down and formulate a plan and decide if we really believe that we could succeed in such an ambitious ploy, bearing in mind that we are talking about the lives of 4,000 of Regby's people and our own lives as well. Is this a justified and achievable risk?"

I quickly replied, "First of all, we need Regby's approval, would he want us to consider making a plan and would he get the support of his people or would we be better employed helping them to get out."

Now all eyes were on Regby who seemed deep in thought.

"I have always made the decisions for my people and I think it only right for me to continue doing so. They have always put their trust in my judgement and I have never let them down."

"My only thoughts are why would you jeopardise yourselves for a group of people your governments would consider as aliens."

The room was silent for several moments before Mukesh suddenly broke the silence and answered Regby's question.

"I am a Hindu and I believe the following: There are five letters in the word Hindu. H stands for honesty, I for integrity, N for nobility, D for devotion, and U stands for unity. Everyone who has those values demands respect and compassion. I believe you have those values and as humans we are duty bound to help you and assist you to live long and noble lives, we would like to help you."

They were eloquent words and we all nodded our agreement.

"If we are going to remain here and help Regby and his people then we need to make a decision about our two colleagues from the Royal Navy, and also Cap'n Joe and the Latis."

Chris, Jimmy and James decided to look at all the entrances to the caves and the possible places that the enemy could gain access.

Whilst they were planning defence strategies Mukesh and I made our way back to the submersible and concocted a story to tell John and Barry that would sound convincing.

Our story was that we needed to spend a number of weeks studying the fauna and rock formations deep underground and that we had also found another entrance and that after one more trip their job would be complete.

Bungy said that he would have liked to have stayed with us but unfortunately his vacation time was coming to an end and he would have to return to Bovisand. He did, however, ask us to keep him in mind for any future events that came up as he was due to leave the Royal Navy in two years' time and he still did not know what he was going to do when he retired from the service.

We needed to return with them to the *Latis* and ask Joe to go shopping for us in Derry. Joe had been getting quite concerned because the weather was deteriorating rapidly and it was approaching the deadliest time of year in the North Atlantic.

Bungy quickly loaded up the fifteen full sets of diving equipment from the *Latis* onto the LR5 and Joe gave us two sets of ship to shore portable radio units to take with us. This would keep us in contact with him at all times.

Joe instructed John and Barry to deliver everything to us quickly and return to the *Latis* so that he could return to Derry to sit out the coming storm. He said that he hoped to return to the area within three to four weeks when hopefully the spell of bad weather would have subsided a little. We gave him a shopping list and he looked rather quizzical as he looked it over.

As many large containers of Vaseline as possible, forty lengths of 4" x 4" wood suitable for shoring, ten high pressure fireman's hoses, two high pressure portable water pumps and whatever explosives he could get his hands on. A twenty pound bag of 6 inch nails, some twine and some fine gauge netting.

Joe laughed and commented, "Looks more like you are controlling a riot rather than going on a caving expedition."

You have no idea Joe, I thought, you have no idea. I surmised that Joe was very close to the truth although he had only said it in jest.

In the meantime Chris, Jimmy and James were getting a full tour of the cave system as Regby showed them the access points from the surface. Chris was looking at various vantage points where they could surprise and attack the enemy and James was measuring all the dimensions near to the entrance of the system.

Jimmy employed himself checking out how much light came in from outside and searching all of the adjacent passageways to ascertain if apertures could be made from them into the main entrance way and unseen from it. He found one that ran completely parallel to the right of the main entrance as you entered and another directly beneath the main entrance. Neither of these was more than five feet way and apertures could be punched through from them for access.

Regby informed them that there were other small entrances but Chris said that these could be completely sealed so that the attacking Annunaki would only have one option of entering Regby's labyrinth. They then went into the accommodation area of the Regby's clan.

Here for the first time they came face to face with the womenfolk and children. They were extremely nervous for a while but relaxed after Regby had explained quickly that these were friends who had come to help protect them from the enemy.

The women kept at a safe distance still wary of these strange people who had come into their underground world; however the children were far more curious and acted much like our own inquisitive children.

The womenfolk were even smaller than their men and would have been about four feet eight inches tall. They had tiny pixie like faces and their blond hair wrapped around their delicate faces. Each one of them had piercing emerald green eyes that were totally captivating. They were all very petite and none of them showed signs of any obesity. I put this down to their very healthy seafood and vegetable diet.

The children of Babillu were almost clones of their mothers, and the males did not really start to develop muscles and masculine features until they were about fifteen years old when their small frames filled out and they grew several inches over a period of just a couple of years.

Chris said that he felt it was the children who with their childlike trust had breached the gap between us and them. They were quick to make friends and so curious that they followed us everywhere we went. There were a few differences between them and our children but they were still children and acted the way that you would expect children to act.

The only problem was that they all looked a lot younger than they really were because of their tiny stature. Ten year old children compared in size with a human child of about five years; nevertheless they were still children.

Brendan was fascinated by the technology in the library and said he would like to spend some time in there. Grace accompanied him, and Regby instructed the librarian to help and advise them in whatever they wanted. Brendan believed that it would be possible to replicate most of the technology apart from the telepathy aspect which would be something that would not be attainable for many years, if ever.

It took Mukesh and me most of the day to move the diving sets along the passageways and into the city. Chris and I also set up the ship to shore radio aerial high above the main entrance to the cave and facing the south.

The weather had deteriorated. A full blown storm developed and we were wondering how Joe was coping out in that atrocious weather. Joe had heard their radio call, but was far too busy trying to keep the *Latis* facing into the wind and stopping it from breaching.

Joe later told us that it was the worst weather he had ever encountered. He was tossed like a cork and mountainous waves were crashing over the bows and completely obscuring his view. Many times he had to fight the ship back on course and he wondered if he would survive in the swirling maelstrom. *Latis* had to battle up to twenty foot seas and wind gusts up to sixty knots. He heard the awful rending sounds as the storm battered *Latis* juddered and fought her way to keep afloat.

Only once did he venture onto the upper deck to try and assess the damage but the wind and freezing rain cut through to his skin and he lost his footing and was nearly washed over the side. He had to crawl back on his hands and knees to the bridge.

Many fittings had been stripped away from the deck of his ship before he finally limped into Derry. He arrived just about in one piece but with a lot of upper deck damage and his body was battered and bruised. He had lost both of the safety sea-boats and nearly all of the light fittings had been torn away. He had lost an anchor and he believed that James's reinforcement of the deck and bows had saved his life and ensured the survival of his beloved *Latis*.

The *Latis* was in a sorry state but still in one piece. There was a lot of work to be done to get her ready to return to Surtsey and he knew it was going to be a lot longer than he had anticipated. However, he got a team of shipwrights in immediately and they set about repairing the damage. There was quite a lot of water in the bilges and the bilge pumps had overheated and burnt out trying to keep the leaks under control.

He left the shipwrights to get on with the work on *Latis*, and then made his way to the harbour masters office because he knew that he would have to try and contact me and let me know what had happened. He made a radio telephone call to the harbour master at Reykjavik and asked if he would call Surtsey on the ship to shore radio and let them know the plight of the *Latis* and that Joe would be late returning.

Reykjavik called and gave us the news of Joe and the *Latis* and asked if we needed a rescue boat to come and pick us up. I told the harbourmaster that we would be alright, and that we had a lot of work to do and we would hang on until Joe managed to get *Latis* repaired and return to us.

There was a lot of work to be done and although the equipment that Joe had was really needed, we could do a lot of the work without it.

First of all we needed to make sure that the women and children of Regby's clan would be safe from harm when the attack came, and allocated them homes at the far end of Babillu, most of which nestled higher than the rest of the homes. These could accommodate over 2,000 people which would keep them well protected.

The rest of them would need to take refuge in the library and to that end we all set about making it secure. All the doors to the front and side of the building were made completely watertight using an Annunaki cloth which was a mixture of a metallic substance and some sort of plastic. It was extremely durable and completely waterproof.

The 100 suits that they had used to get everyone into the cave system were still in good condition as they had been kept in a state of repair in the event that they would be needed again. This was one such time that they would certainly needed.

Chris then instructed Regby to select his best men who would be up to the task of assisting with the defence of their people.

Those selected would have their bodies completed smothered in Vaseline to prevent any moisture reaching their skin and then they would wear the all in one protective metallic suits.

When the explosives arrived, Chris and Jimmy would set them to explode and fill all the entrances to the tunnel except one and in the meantime all of our team went above ground to start to try and camouflage the smaller entrances. The idea was to keep the main entrance open and visible but also to restrict the number of people who could enter at the same time.

There were a lot of loose lumps of volcanic rock and shale to move and the mammoth task began to prepare for an attack.

Whenever he could Brendan and Grace slipped back into the library to continue their study of all of the technology that the Annunaki had. Brendan also told Grace that as soon as Joe arrived and they had offloaded the goods from the *Latis* he wanted her to go with Joe and get herself back to University. She would probably be able to get a flight from Reykjavik directly back to London.

Despite her protests he insisted that she went. He prepared a letter to send back with her explaining that the weather had been atrocious and she was unable to return on time and that he was truly sorry for Grace being late back. He knew that Lisa would need to be called and told of the situation and that we were all OK. Until then there was still a lot of work to be done.

Back in the cave entrance in which we had arrived, James and I managed to loosen a few rocks close to the original cave in and very soon the passageway was completely blocked once more, so securing one more possible area of threat.

There was little more we could do now until the *Latis* arrived and so we set about training the women and children and those who would be in the library to get into their safety positions as quickly as possible.

They all had places to go and the first couple of times they tried the evacuation procedure it was total chaos. Chris soon had everyone well trained so that in the end all of them were able to stop whatever they were doing and evacuate in less than twenty-five minutes. He started off by making them do it every day just after they had eaten breakfast. Later, as they became more proficient, he would do it at odd times of the day and night without any prior warning. He used four whistles for the warning sign, with four of us standing in a predetermined spot and all blowing the whistles at the same time. It was very effective.

Christmas came and went but there was no celebration because there was too much to do and anyway the Annunaki did not celebrate this religious festival. All of us were now starting to get keyed up and nervous about the events of the future. We had no idea when or how the attacks would be only that we expected them before or during the spring season.

At one stage Chris contemplated putting explosives underwater around the entrance to the cave but gave up on that idea after some consideration. One thing was that we did not know exactly how they would arrive and also he subsequently believed that the best deterrent was to allow them access and hit them when they themselves were trapped in the confines of the cave.

We were getting used to the variety of seafood that we had and the vegetables were varied and nutritious. Grace, who always tried to eat sensibly, agreed that this was a first class diet and had all the right ingredients to keep them healthy. She missed her gym workouts but scrambling around on the rocks and through the passageways was a great cardio vascular exercise. Also our heart rate was on a permanent high because of the situation we were in. I am not sure that all the stress was too good.

After dinner in the evenings we would all sit together, including Regby and those he had chosen to assist in the defence, whilst Chris and Jimmy outlined the plan.

We had no idea of the numbers that would be coming in the attack but there was only room for two or three at a time to enter and they could be easily picked off as they came in.

From the adjacent passageways and also from below the hoses would be used to pump in salt water under pressure, hopefully destroying them as they came. This would certainly create panic and mayhem amongst the attackers and they would back off. This would only be the beginning because they would regroup and come up with another plan and we had to be ready for all contingencies.

The next part would be above the main entrance if they got through the entrance passage. A huge tank would be built with James providing the shoring to hold it in place. The tank would be prepared by the Annunaki women out of the metallic, plastic substance. James worked out the approximate size he required and the work on this commenced immediately.

It was surprising but the time passed by very quickly and there was a huge amount of activity going on all the time as each member prepared to carry out his or her tasks. Mealtimes became a social event and more and more frequently this took place out along the main street of the city instead of inside their homes. It reminded me of the way the village people around the Mediterranean enjoyed communal meals.

We were getting nervous and tense, and we needed Joe to return very soon. We were become very concerned that he might be too late. At last, on a bright sunny morning with a relatively calm sea the *Latis* anchored about 250 yards away from our position. It was January 17th 2090 and he was a sight for sore eyes. Everyone was so pleased to see him.

Regby and his clan kept well out of sight, still very frightened of other beings apart from us. Joe only thought we were on an expedition and so we did not want to alter his perceptions.

Although the weather was good there was a heavy swell and it was quite dangerous and also time consuming getting all of the stores that Joe had brought for us off the *Latis*.

The wooden shores were brought off first and without any further ado James started building the framework for the improvised tank. Mukesh helped him and passed the shores and rope up to him and then climbed up to assist in tying them all in situ.

By the time we had retrieved everything from the boat, Mukesh and James were near to completing the tank shelf. They had to leave one end open until the tank was up and then they could secure that end as well.

We sent Grace and Joe off to the nearby beach of Vic about 100 miles from Reykjavik to await our instructions. Grace would make her way from there back to London. Joe told us to take our time as he had friends here in Iceland and always enjoyed his visits.

He told us that during one really bad winter he had spent nearly three months stranded in Iceland, and that once he was off the Atlantic Ocean the weather conditions were not too cold and certainly no colder than Derry in winter.

The next few days were a hive of activity with the sound of hammers and sawing and firing up motors and small explosions. By the time we had finished preparing everything our ears were ringing from the continuous noise; nevertheless we were pleased to have it completed.

Chris kept disappearing with Jimmy, always on the lookout for other opportunities. They spent a lot of time down by the underground river that cascaded down through the roof of the cave. Chris used a diving set and Jimmy tended him on a lifeline as he climbed up through the cavity through which the river flowed. He pushed and pulled himself against the huge torrent of water higher and higher into the rock.

Chris then gave us the details of what he had found and how it could be used to our advantage. The street leading up into the city was uphill and therefore there was no danger of flooding. The entrance to the cave was slightly downhill which meant that any water spilled into the cave would automatically exit down through the entrance.

A small explosion in the rock face upstream of the river would blow a hole through the rock and the full force of the river would rush straight out through the entrance forcing anything in its path back out and into the ocean.

It seemed most unusual that the river could be coming in higher than the ocean and that it was also mostly fresh water, also it was not cold.

Just out of curiosity Chris wanted to follow the course of the river and try and find its source. This time, with Jimmy accompanying him, he re-entered the river and with both of them in full diving gear they forced themselves along its course. After about 250 yards, and somewhere behind the accommodation end of the city, they came out into a large warm steamy cavern.

Chris said that the visibility was so low that it was like being in a Turkish steam room. They had found the source of the river; a geyser of hot fizzing bubbling water was jetting under pressure into the cavern and after cascading off the roof was dropping back and forming the river that we had navigated.

We didn't have to worry about the water running out.

"Night vision goggles," said James suddenly.

"What?"

"Night vision goggles," he repeated,

"Why didn't I think of it before, we need night vision glasses."

"Of course I should have thought of it as well. You're absolutely right, James, they could make the difference between success and failure," said Chris.

"I wonder if they have any in Iceland," I said. "I'll call Joe and see if he can get some quickly."

I immediately called Joe on the ship to shore radio and he went off to see if he could get some straight away. I told him that we had come across some small rodents in the caves and if we used lights they wouldn't come out. It was the only thing I could think of without raising any suspicion.

Good old Joe, he was back on the radio within less than an hour to say, "How many do you need?"

I glanced at Chris who said that forty would be good but then realised if we asked for too many then Joe would know that we had more people than just our team.

"There are five of us," I said, "So perhaps we ought to double that figure to ten in the event of any accidents."

Joe then replied that they come in cases of thirty and it would be the cheapest way to buy them. I smiled to myself and agreed with him and could he bring them as soon as possible.

"Why does Iceland have so many night vision goggles?" I asked him.

"Well, most of the winter Iceland is in total darkness, as you may have noticed and they are almost standard equipment up here in the arctic."

"I guess they would be," I replied, "I hadn't really thought about it."

"Instead of up anchoring and coming over I will bring them in a sports boat that one of my trawler buddies owns, it will be a lot quicker and easier."

"Thanks Joe," I replied. "See you in a little while."

Chapter 23 The Finale

The night vision goggles arrived and James checked them all out and issued a pair to everyone involved with the immediate defence of the caves.

Regby appeared looking very worried. “I have just thought of a serious flaw in our planning,” he said. “It isn’t something that the Annunaki would need to worry about but humans are very vulnerable.”

“What do you mean?” said Chris.

“As you already know, Annunaki are telepathic which means our enemy will be able to scan your thoughts. We have the ability to block them out but you can’t.”

“How close do they have to be to be able to brain scan?” I asked Regby.

“Up to about forty feet,” he replied.

“Can they use telepathy through rock?” I asked him.

“Yes, but it can reduce the distance although I couldn’t give you any specific details.”

"Regby can you work with your scientists and engineers and see if you can think of something that will cloak their telepathy."

Nearly everything was ready for the attack and we had begun to take it in turns wearing the night vision goggles to keep a look out for the enemy. The light inside the caves was kept to a minimum and when the attack came all light would be extinguished.

Regby and his technical team worked around the clock to try and come up with a solution to block the telepathy. They tried sound waves, radio waves and a dozen other ideas including music but nothing seemed to work.

Then I had an idea, "What is the material that is being used for protection against the water made of?" I asked Regby.

"It is a metal, plastic and fibre mix," he replied.

"Can we try making a head covering and see if it has any blocking effect on the telepathy?" I asked Regby.

After tests on all of us there was a reduction of telepathy distance of about ten per cent; this was not enough but it was a move in the right direction. I asked Regby if the material mix could be altered. "Of course," he replied.

I then left Regby to carry on testing different compositions, asking him to come up with the right mix.

That night we thought that the attack was on when a dark shadowy silhouette silently approached the beach. Using the goggles we could clearly see the craft getting closer to the shore. It seemed very small and we wondered if it was an advance party come to scour the area.

The small boat crunched onto the volcanic beach and seemed to make a great deal of noise as the occupants jumped onto the black gravel. Then we could hear giggling as a couple of young lovers appeared, walking hand in hand along the beach.

It was a very cold night and they were both wearing arctic cagoules to keep out the bitter cold. Even though they were keeping warm it was very dangerous to attempt such a feat at night in the middle of winter. The wind could whip up in a matter of seconds and they would easily be swept away and lost at sea.

Chris was quick thinking and shouted at them. "What are you doing here? This is a private conservation area. Please return to the mainland immediately."

"Sorry, we didn't know," they shouted back in broken English. Then the couple ran back to their boat and were soon heading back to the mainland.

Regby and his technical team worked hard on finding the right combination of materials that would effectively block the telepathy and eventually came up with the most effective mix that they could. Telepathy could only work at a close range of less than ten feet. We would have to live with it and make sure that we kept the enemy at a safe distance.

We had planned everything down to the last detail and now the tension was beginning to mount. It was the middle of February and we knew that the time for an attack was coming nearer by the day. The opposing Annunaki needed to flush out and destroy Regby and his clan within the next two or three weeks, before the next contingent of immigrants arrived from Nibiru.

Another big storm hit Surtsey with huge waves crashing over the beaches. A lot of debris was thrown up onto the shore and it looked as if another boat had met with disaster. However amongst the debris were some sheets of metal and we carried these back into the caves. I called Regby and asked him to come and look at our find.

He confirmed my suspicions that this was indeed Annunaki metal and what had been washed up was part of the convoy of vessels coming in for the attack. This was both good and bad news. The good news was that there was one less vessel but the bad news was that they were close by. Now we would have to be extra vigilant.

By early the following day several bodies had been washed up onto the beach and they were without any doubt Annunaki. The length of their bodies gave it away but they were very badly mutilated, the salt water had taken a heavy toll on their features and they were completely unrecognisable. Now we knew what the water could do.

There was no place to bury the bodies and we knew that we couldn't let them be discovered by anyone else and so we placed them close to the water and set fire to them. Within a couple of hours there was little left but a few ashes and we washed those into the sea.

Two days later, and in the early morning at about 5am, we sighted a vessel approaching the shore. It was still completely dark and without the goggles we would not have seen anything. As it was we could see everything as clear as day. The vessel inched its way behind a promontory about 150 yards from our main entrance.

We left Jimmy guarding the entrance, and Chris and I climbed up high so that we could see what the interlopers were up to. There were fifteen of them and we presumed that they must have been an advance party. At the sight of them I could feel my heart rate rise and that awful sick dread feeling well up inside me. I started to sweat and although Chris remained calm I could see that he was also starting to get agitated at the sight of them.

Were they just sent in to reconnoitre or were they going to try us out and see if we were a soft target? Either way, if they came into the cave they would be in serious trouble.

They were completely silent and it was obvious that they were not sure exactly where to find us. They split up into three different groups and one group went directly inland while the other two groups went in opposite directions along the beach. We moved slowly and quietly back to the entrance and watched and waited to see what they planned to do next. I could feel my legs starting to tremble at the very thought of them getting close and felt violently sick.

After about an hour, one of their groups came very close to our position and it was obvious from their animated gesticulations that they knew that they had found the right place. From where we were viewing we could see them marking our position. Then they left and after scouting around for a few minutes disappeared back along the beach in the direction from which they had come.

Once again we left the relative safety of the cave and followed them back to where they had arrived on the beach. The other two teams were already there waiting. They must have left their waterproof suits on the beach and they quickly donned them on. They remained all together for about twenty minutes before making a mark on the beach and then embarking back onto their boat and disappearing out to sea.

Chris looked at me and said, “Are you alright, Petrey?”

I let go a huge sigh. “I am now Chris, but I am relieved to see them go. Is that feeling of abject fear always going to be there whenever we see them,” I asked him.

He didn't reply but just breathed heavily and I could see he was also very relieved.

Although it was only February there was quite a dull light throughout the day and I did not think they would attempt to launch themselves upon us during daylight hours. Nevertheless after returning to what was now our home, albeit temporarily, we left someone to guard the entrance. Nothing more happened that day.

It was a little after midnight and the night was as black as coal with not a star visible in the sky when a dark shape was once again sighted approaching the shoreline, this time a little closer to the entrance than yesterday morning. Jimmy and Mukesh were in the passageway that lay to the side of the main entrance and James was in the passageway below. All of them had the pressure hoses attached to the quietly running pumps and ready to fire.

Chris and I remained out of sight behind a rock pillar to the left of the entrance so that we could monitor their approach. They came stealthily on until they were close to where we were hiding. We then slipped back into the cave entrance to warn our team of the impending attack.

The City of Babillu was in total darkness and there was total silence inside the cave. Each second seemed like an hour as blood from our increased heartbeats thundered in our heads. I could feel myself beginning to shake again, and I had to prop myself up against the wall of the cave to prevent myself from collapsing in fright.

From our vantage point, and with our night vision goggles, their features became crystal clear as they approached the entrance. They were nothing like Regby's clan, who were somehow gentle and serene looking. These hostile aggressors looked like monsters, ugly, angry and terrifying, their faces grotesque and hideous. All of this just added to my own torment as they approached.

Chris and I quickly moved to a position adjacent to our overhead water tank, ready at a second's notice to drop this huge tank of water onto the advancing Annunaki.

The entered the cave quickly and silently and were already ten feet inside the entrance when Chris gave the instruction.

"NOW," he shouted and the hoses came on simultaneously. James cut off their retreat whilst Jimmy and Mukesh blasted them from the side. The chaos and pandemonium that broke out next was horrific.

They were taken completely by surprise and in their sheer terror and pain tried to turn and get out of the cave. The water blasted and lacerated their susceptible bodies and this coupled with the total darkness just added to their panic as they screamed in mortal pain and fell all over each other. In just a few minutes they lay on the floor, one or two still writhing but mostly deathly still.

We worked quickly to remove the carcasses from the entrance. Most were so badly mutilated that it was impossible to make out any of their features. In many cases the skin was still peeling back and the smell from their burns caught like acid in our throats. I could feel the bile rising within me and had to rush outside to be violently sick. I was not alone and I could see both Mukesh and James retching uncontrollably a few yards away.

Fortunately Regby brought in some of his people to carry on the job of removing the remaining bodies and very soon there were few signs of what had happened.

We knew that this was not the end but only the beginning and wondered how long it would be before the rest of Inanna's

Annunaki would arrive. He would be waiting for his advance party to return, and when they didn't - how would he react? Would it be another stealthy approach or would it be an all-out assault? We could only wait in fear and trepidation.

The women of Babillu prepared a meal for us. About twenty hours had lapsed since we had last had any food but after what had happened and what we had seen, none of us could stomach eating at all.

All five of us were mentally and physically exhausted, and we needed to try and get some sleep, although I doubted any of us would dare to sleep. Regby and his chosen team stood guard whilst we tried to at least rest for a while.

I did manage to drift off for a little while but my mind was in turmoil and the nightmares that accompanied the sleep were horrific. All the horrors and the experiences down the South African mine and tonight's brutal foray all melded into one deeply disturbing and terrifying experience.

I was running away, and yet I was going nowhere, and the apparitions in my nightmare were getting forever closer; I was suddenly wide awake and in a cold sweat as I shivered. I knew I was close to breaking point and wondered how much more of this I could take.

I tried to pull myself together and remember that I had brought the others into this awful situation and I must see if they were all coping with it. None of them had really slept and they were all suffering from food and sleep deprivation and the awful horrors that we had endured with the thought of even more to come.

If we survived this chapter in our lives I vowed to myself that I would never, ever leave home again unless it was on a holiday with my family.

The hoses were checked and rechecked, and the excess water on the floor was dried up. As the hours slipped by the stark memories started to fade just a little bit? We all managed to eat a small amount of food although it was difficult to digest and it appeared to have no taste and I could still taste the acrid bile in my throat.

For two days nothing happened and we all wanted an end to the misery that haunted us. The frustration of it was overwhelming as it appeared we were waiting for our doom. Even Chris, who was usually cheerful and in control, became listless and moody, and kept pacing up and down like a caged animal. Mukesh sat silently and spoke to no-one, Brendan disappeared back into the library to study some more of the technology but I suspect it was to hide himself away with his private terror. Jimmy seemed to be coping better than anyone and spent his time trying to converse with Regby and his close aides.

I felt separate from them all, detached, as if I was not part of all the horror but viewing it from a different place. I knew it was my mind's mechanism for self-defence kicking in and protecting me.

All of a sudden they were there. They had landed on the far side of the island hidden from our view. At the last minute we caught sight of them through our night vision goggles. There were so many of them that it was impossible to count them.

Was this it, was this where it all ended, would we be destroyed or taken captive by these awful creatures that created death and mayhem wherever they went?

We had a distinct advantage, despite the numbers; they still had to come through the entrance which was restricted and only had room for about three of them at a time. We were also aware of their great number and we needed to fell the first ones who came in so that they became an obstacle for those following behind.

The stealthy approach ended at the entrance; as they came upon us there was a cacophony of sound as they squealed and shouted with blood curdling noises enough to awaken the dead. This was a tactic to scare us but somehow it became unreal, and as the heat of the battle commenced, a survival instinct kicked in. I knew we were in a battle for our lives and those of Regby and his people.

As the water cannon fired on them, once more the chilling sound of pain and terror could be heard. For a second I almost felt sorry for them but that didn't last as I knew that it was either us or them. My will and instinct to survive was increased as the adrenaline pumped through my veins.

The writhing bodies on the floor were screaming in pain as the hordes still pouring into the cave fell over them. They kept on coming, some of them badly burnt by the water and some barely touched by it. They swarmed into the main cavern. James had managed to sprint from his position by his water cannon and slashed the rope holding the water in the overhead tank. There was a split second's delay before the water cascaded down in torrents onto the bodies of Inanna's attacking Annunaki. The screams were primeval as they were dashed to the floor of the cave by the sheer weight of water. They lay there concussed and burning from their drenching.

Suddenly, they were in retreat, running, falling, slipping, terrified and screaming in agony as they all desperately tried to exit the cave. Again as they hurtled through the entrance passage the water cannon finished off the job that had been started just a few minutes before.

Just twenty minutes after it had started, the battle was all over with only about twenty of Inanna's army escaping the confines of the cave. Their bodies were later found strewn over the volcanic beach as they tried to retreat to the boats. They were horrifically burnt and had died in excruciating pain.

Inanna was not amongst the dead and Regby said that she must have remained safe away from the action. A true indication of what a cowardly vicious bully she was to send her henchmen in to carry out her foul deeds whilst she remained safe and away from trouble.

Regby was certain now that Inanna would not return. She would have been devastated that not one of her army had returned to report back to her. She had lost an immense battle and would now slink back to her underground lair to lick her wounds.

Amazingly not one of us or Regby's Annunaki was injured in the attack.

We had not had to detonate the explosives that would have blasted the river into the cavern and washed the invaders back into the sea. It would be there in the event of a future attack.

For the next few days we all worked alongside Regby and his people to clear up the mess that the battle had caused and remove all the bodies. A huge funeral pyre was ignited and all of the bodies were destroyed and the stench of burning flesh permeated the air for days.

When the clearing up was completed, everyone from the city came out to greet us. The women and children seemed so grateful for what we had done and we felt humble and pleased that we had been able to save them from a huge tragedy.

The children surrounded Mukesh and were all talking and laughing and all trying to touch him. They all looked so very young because of their small stature. Mukesh looked like a proud father amongst all those grateful children.

Jimmy was in his element, chatting excitedly to the ladies of the clan even though they did not understand a word he was saying.

Brendan was talking to the engineers and scientists in the library, trying to glean the last few dregs of technology before we had to leave. They gave him a few plates for him to study back in his own laboratory. He would be able to reverse engineer the plates and reproduce his own prototype.

James was showing a group of young Annunaki males how to construct wood shores and how to tie secure knots that would not slip but could also be easily loosened if needed.

Chris had another group of young men and was showing them how the hoses and pumps worked. He also collected all of the night vision goggles and gave them a full demonstration before handing them over.

I was talking to Regby to finalise everything because this would be our last evening together.

"Regby, will I ever be able to find out if my Uncle Carl is still alive?" I asked.

"I don't know, Petrey, but if I can find out I will find a way to let you know."

I told him about Emio in Washington and his desperate desire to find out about their metallic substance. I told him about the discoveries found in the mountains in Namibia, China and various other locations and that their secrecy may not last for ever.

Our last night with the Annunaki was a truly memorable one and not one I will ever forget. They cooked us a banquet fit for royalty and Regby stood up and gave an eloquent speech, thanking us for saving his life and those of his people who were precious and dear to him.

Finally, each one of us promised never to divulge any details of them or their whereabouts to anyone other than those who already knew, which included Grace and Lisa.

It was a sad and poignant moment when we bade farewell to these gentle Annunaki making a promise to them that should they ever need us again we would come immediately.

Joe and the *Latis* were waiting.